NEW DIRECTIONS 39

N D

New Directions in Prose and Poetry 39

Edited by J. Laughlin

with Peter Glassgold and Frederick R. Martin

A New Directions Book

Copyright © 1979 by New Directions Publishing Corporation
Library of Congress Catalog Card Number: 37-1751 (Serial)

ACKNOWLEDGMENTS
Walter Abish's "Self-Portrait" (Copyright © 1977 by Walter Abish) was originally included in *Individuals: Post-Movement Art in America*, published by E. P. Dutton.

For "Poems by Poets from Africa," grateful acknowledgment is made to the editors and publishers of books and magazines in which some of the poems previously appeared: for Onyegbule C. Uzoaru, *Nimrod* (Copyright © University of Tulsa, 1977); for Okot p'Bitek, *Song of Lawino*, published by East African Publishing House, Nairobi; for Chinweizu, *Energy Crisis and Other Poems* (Copyright © 1978 by Chinweizu), published by Nok Publishers, International, Lagos and New York; for Ifeanyi Menkiti, *The Jubilation of Falling Bodies* (Copyright © 1978 by Ifeanyi Menkiti), published by The Pomegranate Press, *Stony Brook*, and *Chelsea* (Copyright © 1971 by Chelsea Associates, Inc.); for Christopher Okigbo, *Labyrinths with Path of Thunder* (© 1971 Legal Personal Representatives of Christopher Ikigbo); for Kofi Awoonor, *The House by the Sea* (Copyright © 1978 by Kofi Awoonor), published by Greenfield Review Press.

Quoted passages on "Marsupials," in Christine L. Hewitt's story "Twins," are reprinted from Volume 11 of the *New Encyclopedia Britannica* by permission of the publishers.

Howard Stern's "The Big Orange" ("Rhythm Study II") previously appeared in *Contemporary Quarterly* (© 1976 by Forman Publications).

"Tributes to Louis Zukofsky" are reprinted from the Zukofsky number of *Paiduma* (Volume 7, Number 3), courtesy of the National Poetry Foundation, University of Maine at Orono (Copyright © 1977 by the National Poetry Foundation, Inc.).

Manufactured in the United States of America
First published clothbound (ISBN: 0-8112-0730-7) and New Directions Paperbook 484 (ISBN: 0-8112-0731-5) in 1979

New Directions Books are published for James Laughlin
by New Directions Publishing Corporation,
80 Eighth Avenue, New York 10011

CONTENTS

Walter Abish
 Self-Portrait   1

Gregory Corso
 Feelings on Growing Old   143

Bram Dijkstra
 Seven Poems   88

Carlos Drummond de Andrade
 Song for That Man of the People, Charlie Chaplin   51

Jaime Gil de Biedma
 Eight Poems   26

Ivan Goll
 The Chapliniad   40

Christine L. Hewitt
 Twins   114

Dawson Jackson
 Faust and His World of Plastic   137

J. Laughlin
 The Person   179

Hugh Kenner, Celia Zukofsky, and David Gordon, eds.
 Tributes to Louis Zukofsky   147

Ifeanyi Menkiti, ed.
    Poems by Poets from Africa   95

Joe Ashby Porter
    In the Mind's Eye   63

Howard Stern
    Four Collages   36

Notes on Contributors   180

SELF-PORTRAIT

WALTER ABISH

I

Each day, each hour, passports, marriage licenses, driving licenses, bankbooks, credit cards authenticate the existence of another *I*, although with what amounts to great circumspection the *I* is never referred to in any of these documents that function as signifiers, attributing to each individual a gender, a first and a last name, occasionally an initial for a middle name, as well as a name for each parent, a place of residence, an occupation, also political affiliation, credit rating, criminal convictions, if any, race, religion, education, and age. Frequently the *I* scrutinizes these joyless documents for hours, boxed in and burdened by a proof that is at one. and the same time remote and intolerably near.

An individual will use language to give shape to his *I*. Language unlike a document permits the *I* to unfold, it gives it a freedom to seek out the words that will define its intention and its direction. It does not take long for an individual to discover that there is no need to stress the *I* when saying: I choose not to, or, I couldn't care less, or, I intend to take a walk around the park without you. The recipient of the remark is able to place the *I* addressing him in a proper perspective. Not to be overlooked in some tortured statement is an *I* that stands in a state of solitary and nervous

1

uncertainty in regard to the words that have preceded it and to the words that are to follow. This precarious state of uncertainty is sufficient to crush the I, and obliterate it temporarily. Of course the I can always mobilize words to its defense, but they may not be the right words, the correct words for the occasion. Michel Leiris in *L'Age d'Homme*[1] chooses his words carefully as he with meticulous care magnifies the worries of the I: the hands thin and rather hairy, the veins distinct, the two middle fingers curving inward toward the tip. He seems to believe that the curve of his middle fingers denotes something weak or rather evasive in his character. He may even be correct. He is simply describing his I. Apparently the head is a bit too large for the body, the legs too short, shoulders too narrow, etc. . . . As a reader one is overwhelmed by the seeming preciseness of his dispassionate self-appraisal. The reader is not only overwhelmed, he is also, I venture to think, won over to the degree that he himself lacks Leiris's ability to articulate the flaws that so profoundly cripple his I. I am not suggesting that this is Leiris's objective. All the same, the reader is won over by the disarming candor that the I of Leiris exudes. Possibly if the reader were to see the rather impressive long list of Leiris's achievements he or she might be less likely to accept the merciless self-scrutiny of Leiris's I and say: Well, I don't know . . . where is he leading me? And it is true, the moment the I is inserted in a sentence, the recipient of the statement or remark is being led somewhere . . .

Advancing or retreating the I camouflages itself behind circumlocutionary statements, endowing its small lies, its puny lies, its irrelevant lies with a shine, a polish, a misleading brilliance . . . The I lies at the least provocation, unnecessarily, for no other reason than to state: *I am not really what I seem to you,* or the opposite. *I am the way you see me now, in absolute control, and although I lead a life not too dissimilar from yours, I am far more intelligent and far more successful than you. I have only to press this button and a private elevator will shoot up to this floor* . . . Without a first person what need would there be for language? The I anchors the words firmly to the ground. Lacking the I, speech would lose its plausibility and its intent. From the moment

[1] *Manhood: A Journey from Childhood into the Fierce Order of Virility,* trans. Richard Howard (New York: Grossman Publishers, 1963).

a child begins to speak, its I, once it arrives at the I, faces nameless hurdles and barricades that are invisible to others. It is as if these obstacles exist for one purpose only, to impede the I. It is hardly surprising that the I, under the circumstances, keeps a sharp lookout for what lies ahead . . . how it is being received by others . . . its memory retaining for far too long each gaffe, each hideous irrevocable error, each momentous blunder.

Every time a person opens his mouth to speak his I is standing on the precipice of a bottomless abyss. One single wrong note and the I will take a desperate plunge . . . yet, for hours at a time, the I is also capable of obliterating the excruciating memory of past incidents, as it cheerfully babbles away, completely oblivious of itself, feeling only a delightful sense of harmony, a sense of being in tune with everything that surrounds it. I think the evening went rather well, the I says a bit smugly to whoever happens to be in its vicinity. So much depends on the answer, on the appropriate facial gesture. The slightest miscalculation might cause the I to withdraw into itself, manifesting on the exterior surface a patient resignation until its rage tears that surface apart. There are fortunately ways the I can alleviate its torments. For instance: five hours of TV or any randomly chosen double feature at the local movie house, or even a book might do the trick, allowing the I to resuscitate itself by immersing its I in the attractive flatness of a story line on the screen or page . . . there is also always sex. As it fucks the I is temporarily expunged, only to reassert itself afterward, a bit feebly, it is true, as it addresses the other, saying: I love you. Yet in surfacing the I can only extend as far as the fingertips. One might reason from this that in order to love the I has to be dropped.

The mirror in the bathroom and in the bedroom burden the I with additional information. Being familiar, the information is in certain respects utterly redundant. The I has already seen what it now sees for the thousandth time. Still the I dissects itself with a compulsive passion. It is a bit disheveled in appearance . . . a bit worn . . . fatigued bags under the eyes . . . unattractive skin . . . Only with the greatest courage will the I use a second mirror to examine itself from the side. The profile lacks the symmetry of the front, a balance that to some extent minimizes the flaws or defects. Perhaps a brighter shirt or a beard will improve matters.

The *I* has no name for itself. It does not require a name. Yet it responds instantly whenever it hears its name being mentioned or called. Frequently there is a slight mixup. The *I* can be amazingly hostile to people who respond to the same name. A conflict between two *I*'s who share the name Zachary is almost predictable. Dubiously at first, one Zachary stares at the other. One of them will have to give way. One of them will have to stop his *I* from invading the other's body. Ultimately both will realize that the name they are responding to is merely a cipher. Once they acknowledge this fact, every *I* they encounter is a potential Zachary.

I may this once use the first person, says a writer contemplating a new novel. It is entirely instinctual. He doesn't know why he picks the first person. He may not find out until he is halfway through the novel that his *I* really yearns for another writer.

Self-portraits, a game played by the *I* with great zeal, allow it to divulge bit by bit sensations, emotions, incidents from the past, recollections, all linked to the *I* by an elaborate framework, a fabrication that creates the impression that despite evidence to the contrary the richness, the questionable richness, of the past actually permeates the present. When Arrabal in an interview is asked if he likes to be rejected, he replies that it gives him an impression of living. I can only assume that he is referring to the unequivocal needs of his *I*.

Kafka avoided the perils of the *I*. He took refuge behind one of the letters of our alphabet. It so happened that the letter he picked was the initial of his family name, thereby allowing him to retain in his work—work so removed from the understanding of the family—a formal link to the exteriority of his self. His *I* was reserved for his intimate letters to Milena, his long letter to his father that his father never received, his entries in his diaries, and the people with whom he was in daily contact. From what is known about Kafka, one can only deduce that his *I* was a bit too frail to endure the prolonged icy contemptuous tyranny of *The Castle* or *The Trial*. So we are left with the letters, the diaries, Janouch's conversations, and Max Brod's frequently exuberant and optimistic version of Kafka's *I*. Brod refers to Kafka's humor. It is an all too familiar humor.

I am not free tonight, I said to H went she invited me to her place for the first time. How about Saturday? We agreed on Saturday. She found it difficult to pronounce my name in Hebrew. This was years ago in Tel Aviv. By now the Hebrew word for *I* is completely foreign to me. I no longer have any use for it, having left H, having left the country.

A friend recently told me that he has been working on a story titled: "Why I do not write like Franz Kafka."

Will it be in the first person?

Or

The word *or* frequently precedes an alternate proposal. *It's sink or swim.* The imperative to stay above water to a nonswimmer like myself is as unpleasant as the alternative that precedes it. It's only a metaphor, I tell myself. In the English language *or* is frequently coupled with *either*. Kierkegaard wrote a book, fittingly in two volumes, entitled *Either/Or*. Certain details of Kierkegaard's life continue to fascinate me. As a young man he paid excessive attention to his appearance. Wearing his best suit, he would regularly parade up and down the theater district of Copenhagen, for some reason deriving a certain satisfaction whenever people said: There goes Kierkegaard that good for nothing. I imagine that in his mind his love for Regina collided with the words *Either/Or*. On the pretext that he was no longer in love with her he broke off their engagement. In this manner he managed to cling forever to his love, and selfishly devote himself to his writing. I expect that something can be said in favor of inflicting pain upon oneself. It seems by far preferable than having someone else do it who might be less experienced and less skilled at this demanding task. As for Regina. She married, had children, and read all of Kierkegaard's books as soon as they appeared at the local bookstore. Somewhere in each of his books there is contained a message that only she could understand. I have read a few of Kierkegaard's books looking for his message to Regina, but it is well hidden . . .

Sink or swim. Having once almost drowned in a Shanghai swimming pool I cannot hear the word *or* mentioned without feeling a vague trepidation that is only somewhat assuaged when the speaker in question, out of compassion, says: Or else you can leave it the way it is. How reassuring the final *or*. Or you can spend the weekend with us. Or finally you can read *The Sacred Fount*. Or you can fix yourself a light lunch. Or you can take a trip to Central Asia.

Just before she entered a hotel on Montague Street in Brooklyn Heights I overheard a fairly attractive woman tell the man accompanying her: Or you can fuck us both. What, I often wondered, preceded the *or*.

No

I have a tendency to admire people who can easily decline an invitation by simply saying *no*. How easy it seems. No. Not even sorry. Just, No. In a café on Rehov Ben Yehuda the man at the next table said *no* to a couple who had invited him to join them at a party. I overheard him say, *no*. I don't really know why I should remember this particular incident. At that time he and I had not met, although we both frequented the same café and often sat at adjacent tables. His name was Michael Galt. Actually, in retrospect, it was erroneous of me to respect his ability to say *no*, since I now suspect that this gesture may have been made partly for my benefit. Later, when he and I became friends he would always insist on paying every time we went out together. I never once said *no*. Michael lived in a small hotel in the vicinity of Dizengoff Square. Since he left everyone under the impression that he had a good deal of money, I was surprised the first time I saw his small crowded and unattractive hotel room. It's only temporary, he assured me. I find it convenient, I can walk to work. He was an assistant bank manager, but also spoke of working for American Intelligence. I believe I doubted everything he told me. Once, at his urging I visited the bank where he was employed. I was somewhat astonished to discover that indeed he was an assistant bank manager. He was still, given my distrust, determined to prove that he worked for American Intelligence, but that was a more difficult thing to do. We saw each other almost daily. I was incapable of saying *no*. Michael turned everything he did, no matter how trivial, into a kind of ceremony . . . everything became ritualized: the headwaiter's greeting, Michael scanning the menu, and after the meal having coffee served on the terrace, discussing our work, our mutual friends . . . it only dawned on me some time later that I detested Michael. I stopped seeing him. On the telephone he reproachfully said: You don't wish to see me. No, I said. Six months later I ran into him in the company of an old school friend of mine. Where had they met? How did they come to know each other? They had met in Aden, I was told. What were they doing in Aden? A few months later I ran into Michael in the vicinity of his bank. He had been fired that very same day for embezzling large sums of money. He had spent all of it on his friends, he explained. He had been doing it for a couple of years. To his relief the bank had decided not to press charges since he knew a good deal about their dubious business transactions. As far as I could determine he did not change his life-style. He and my friend, for as long as they could, kept on eating in some of the more expensive restaurants. After each meal Michael would sign the bill with a great flourish. He would also add a substantial tip for the waiter. Gradually he had to avoid walking down certain streets in order not to be spotted by people to whom he owed money. He admitted that all this had somewhat jeopardized his work for American Intelligence . . .

I still find it most difficult to say *no,* and therefore use other words to convey the message. My difficulty stems from a certain sympathy I have for the recipient of the *no* . . . yet the *no* is quick and in the long run preferable to the words I choose . . . but one cannot cling to the word *no,* the way one can to words such as: maybe . . . perhaps . . . possibly . . . I'll think of it . . . I'll keep you in mind . . . If the occasion arises . . . you may mention my name if you like . . .

When Michael and I first met he asked me why in the past I had kept staring at him in the café. I could not explain that the way he had been able to say *no* to that extremely attractive couple had caught my attention. I always wanted to meet them, but never did.

I have, however, said *no* under the most unusual circumstances. A few hours after my marriage to H, the wedding took place in a building on lower Allenby Street, she invited me up to her apartment (or was it now legally our apartment?) for a drink, and I said *no.* Perhaps not that abruptly . . . and not in English. After our marriage I would drop by infrequently to visit her. I was always on guard. Always prepared to say *no*. It's such a great pity, she said somewhat sadly the day we were divorced, all those wasted opportunities . . .

There are people dedicated to the *no*. They say *no* on principle. Their faces testify their need to say *no:* ask me anything, and my answer will be *no*. To say *yes* would be to admit a defeat, an unbearable and crushing defeat.

She

In the story or novel the pronoun *she* may well refer to a woman who is young, attractive, and single. For instance, when one reads: "She crossed 57th Street and walking briskly entered the arcade," a vague picture is formed and connected to what preceded that particular sentence. As far as the reader is concerned a certain logic determined the placement of this sentence within the dense forest of words that constitute the entire work. Whether pertinent or not, the sentence forms a connecting link without conspicuously calling attention to itself. The information—it is nothing but information—is recorded by the reader unless he happens to have skipped over that particular line. The woman in question may or may not be young, single and attractive. Whether she's young, single and attractive may be left to the reader to decide. It may not be pertinent as far as the book is concerned. On the other hand, the fact that she is carrying a Pucci handbag could be as relevant as the Legion of Honor rosette in the lapel of Roberte's suit, in the novel *Roberte Ce Soir* by Klossofsky. Klossofsky ingeniously attaches an erotic content to these iconographic emblems . . . an eroticism that pervades the entire text. Frequently the reader, as if participating in a Pavlovian experiment, responds not to the story or novel but to a word or sentence that catches his eye. Almost invariably the pronoun *she* precedes or closely follows the word or sentence which in the reader's brain has acquired a highly charged content. Quite unknowingly the writer has provided a reader with an item of information that is self-contained, that can be lifted from the book, permitting the reader to linger over it as he forms his own anticipatory creation, a fantasy that functions independently of the story or book that initially was its raison d'être. As in fiction our speech is sprinkled with masculine and feminine pronouns. The pronoun *she* is a common occurrence. No one raises an eyebrow. No one is perplexed. The speaker is simply referring to a woman. It could be a passenger speaking to the driver of a bus. She works at the lumberyard, says the passenger. She's a secretary. The passengers within earshot listen to the exchange. They do not know who *she* is. They will never find out. Not infrequently the pronoun *she* is used in the presence of the subject. She's always in bed by twelve, someone might say. And the person being discussed stands silently, feeling that to deny or affirm the statement would only serve as a provocation . . . since, for the duration of that particular exchange, *she* is not present, not counted, completely invisible.

In a book the statement she's a bitch could raise certain expectations in the reader that the author might feel compelled to satisfy. In daily conversation the venom that frequently is attached to a pronoun can disable a man or a woman without any explanation ever forthcoming. To the question, Did you invite Sandra? the response, She's a bloody bitch, may not be inappropriate or surprising. There's no further need to dwell on Sandra.

The pronoun has become a necessity. For each name the brain instantly supplies a pronoun.

I confided to Felix that I intended to marry H, who would otherwise have to join the Israeli army.

What is she like? asked Felix.

Felix absorbs everything I tell him. She's attractive, she has a large apartment in Zaphon-Tel Aviv. She's a terrible cook. She adores Gamzu (a popular Israeli art critic). She detests hiking or going to the beach. She's never read a word I've written.

A few years later without Felix's prompting I painted a more elaborate picture of her. Naturally I also included Felix and myself. I called what I had done a novel. From time to time I changed the novel slightly. I improved it. I interpreted what had happened, and then I interpreted my interpretation. I decided, for instance, that when she had moved her bed to a different part of the room after I left her, her intention had been to erase my former presence. I don't know if that is true. It worked as far as the novel was concerned, and that for a writer remains the chief criterion. A few years ago a mutual friend of ours told me that H had become a judge. How fitting, I thought. In my mind I can see her say: *either/or* as well as *no* without any hesitation. If I ever were to rewrite the novel I might be tempted to include this piece of information. I might even offer a tentative explanation: She became a judge hoping that one day I might appear in front of her in court.

End

Watching a movie we are actually observing a reel of celluloid unwind, frame by frame, across a concentrated beam of light, thereby forming on a large white screen a replication of a life we have come to identify as ours, a life that is expressed by having a couple of people speaking, or fighting, or riding on an old-fashioned train, the motion or immobility of what we see usually being predicated on a story that may have been written by someone who does not know the first thing about making a film. In any event the audience is not unaware that what it is watching is contained frame by frame on the reel, and that there may be two or three or four reels, and that they will have to sit in their seats for approximately one hundred twenty or one hundred forty or one hundred seventy-five minutes in order to see the entire film, and that as the last frame on the last reel crosses the aperture through which the beam of light is being directed, the filmmaker has brought his film, his version of a story or book, his verisimilitude of life to an end. The end of the movie coincides with the end of a reel of film. The end of a peep show on 42nd Street is the end of five or six two-minute segments of voyeurism. Another quarter will in the same machine repeat one of the five or six segments in the cycle detailing the same sexual entanglement. Even the producer of these brief films will adhere to a certain procedure, which acknowledges a beginning and an end. No matter how innovative a chess player Fischer may be, he knows, perhaps to his sorrow, that there is a beginning and an end game and that he must play accordingly. At a certain stage a chess player knows that he has passed the beginning stage and is entering the middle stage and that very soon it will be time to prepare for the ending. At some point both players become aware that they have entered the final stage. They need not communicate this to each other verbally. Although time is a significant element in professional chess, it only accentuates the beginning, the middle, and the end game. The game played without a clock does not change in substance. Clock or no clock the end is anticipated by the players. At the start of the game, reading the first page of a book, or the moment a film begins, the end is brought into play. In chess the fierceness of the end game appears to be more conspicuous because most of the chess pieces have been eliminated. A player who shrinks from methodically destroying a weaker opponent is simply prolonging the game, prolonging the monotony of the checkmate. In the end game a kind of nakedness of intent becomes apparent. Unlike his opponent, the losing player can always resign, thereby bringing the game to an end before the entire game has been played out. The filmmaker can also become a victim of the end. Even a gifted filmmaker like Godard has killed off his major characters at the end. The death of the character coincided with the conclusion of the film. Broadly speaking, the filmmaker, the chess player, and the writer are left with fewer and fewer options as they approach the end. In the mystery film the ending has a definite function, namely to resolve the mystery, point to the killer, and if possible implicate someone who was never under any suspicion. What has been cloudy becomes clear. In *The Fire Within* by Malle the hero commits suicide at the end. Since I had grown attached to him I felt a sense of grief. If I were to see the film again I might conceivably walk out before the end. In *L'Immortell* Robbe-Grillet disoriented the viewer by having his protagonist die an identical death to the mysterious woman he had been following and whose identity he was never able to determine. Both died in the same white convertible, their broken necks twisted at the same angle . . . By repeating every detail of the woman's death, Robbe-Grillet has forced us to shift the end in our minds until we juxtapose it with the death of the woman. The end leads us back into the middle, as Robbe-Grillet to some degree avoided the total confinement of the ending. Kafka in a much more circuitous fashion avoided the end in his then unpublished three novels by simply not completing them. It was left up to Max Brod to provide a quasi end to the three works. Since every move by the protagonist in *Amerika*, *The Trial*, and *The Castle* invites the mounting anxiety that often accompanies the end, the end in itself is almost redundant. It has been stated over and over again. I cannot pick up Kafka, but I read over and over again a story by Borges called *Death and the Compass* which bears a resemblance to the mathematical equation $a + b + c = x$. On first reading the story one is unprepared, accepting at face value the contrivance that entices the detective in the story to move from a to b then to c, finally as surprised as the reader, to die at x. The entire equation flashing in front of our eyes. Six months ago a friend of mine disappeared. A few days before her disappearance she called me up, explaining that she would like to come over and see me. I told her that it was slightly inconvenient since I had some work to finish, but she persisted until I agreed to see her. I now realize that she came not, as I had thought, to speak to me about her problems, but simply to hand me the key to her apartment. A few days later, informed by a mutual acquaintance that she was missing, I went to her apartment searching the place for some clue to her whereabouts. Why else had she given me her key? She had left all her possessions behind. All her books, papers, documents, credit cards, bankbooks. I found the signed copy of my novel in her handbag. This was six months ago. I keep hoping that it was not the *end*. Was she afraid that I might not know of it when it took place.

H and I alternately toyed with the *end* of our relationship. Everything we did lacked conviction . . . I left her, but then under some duress returned. I left her again only to marry her. This time there was no further need to return. The marriage was a sufficient bond. We lived apart. When I looked out of my window and saw her passing on the street below I could always say: There goes my end. Face to face with her I was able to contemplate an *end* that was continuing.

Frequently we would meet at the Niza. She tormented me by mentioning her lover. I prolonged the meetings. Having returned the key to her apartment I could only speculate at the changes that had taken place in her apartment since I had left. If she were to read this, I am convinced she would find what I write absolutely incorrect. Her mind could never tolerate the disturbance my dissatisfaction imposed upon her. By marrying her I was able to withhold the *end*. I was twenty and had not yet read Kafka or Kierkegaard. It was sheer intuition, if you will . . .

Try

To try anything is to leave open an avenue of retreat. In a primitive society the young are uniformly initiated into a communal tribal life. Tribal survival depends largely on the acceptance of established customs and practices and not on experimentation with new ones. At an early age the boys begin practicing with bow and arrow. The bow and arrows are toys only in a manner of speaking. Even the exception in the tribe, the man who becomes a shaman, does not start out by trying, just as the men who carve the totems do not first practice at carving . . . Every move made in a tribe spells out an intention that will be carried out . . .

In our society we are encouraged to try out everything. It is made misleadingly clear to us that everything is more or less available to be tried. There are books that will enable us to build a twenty-foot boat, a transmitter, a Molotov cocktail, or confidently set about publishing our own books. In general, our ability to do things, everyday things, to hop on a bus, hijack a plane, or register at a hotel under an assumed name, has to appear convincing not only to ourselves, but to others too. We do not try it. We do it to test ourselves. Just as we test ourselves every time we fall into a strange bed and find our spontaneous responses to whoever happens to be in the bed closely examined. We strive to feel at ease, quite quite quite relaxed . . . we don't like to admit that we are doing anything for the first time. To try something is basically an attempt to overcome the hurdle of the first time. But how reassuring to know that one can always back out . . . Have you ever lived in a ménage à trois? Try it. Have you ever spent a year with a primitive tribe that still practices cannibalism? Try it. Have you ever fucked a fourteen-year-old in Morocco? Try it. Have you ever crossed the Sahara in a caravan? Try it. Have you ever written a book? Try it.

In a tribe the boundaries are clearly defined, and there is no withdrawal possible from one's place or role within the tribe without endangering the stability of the tribe. The American painter who lived with a tribe of cannibals returns to America and writes a book about it. He is listed in the telephone directory, and I suppose, one could call him up, ask his advice . . . However, intrinsic to certain exploratory situations is the danger that after a certain stage a return is impossible. One can try a sex change, gradually, until . . .

For the less intrepid the plastics industry in America and Japan produces an assortment of devices . . . some replicating what is otherwise sexually unavailable for the purchaser.

If we were to receive a message from outer space that read: Is there any other way to live? Our reply might be: No, there is not, but we try.

Past

Any material that deals with the years 1943 or 1947 can be said to deal with the past. The *I Ching*, which was the subject of a series of lectures by Hellmut Wilhelm in 1943, does not focus attention on the past. The text, at least in the English translation, is firmly rooted in a kind of permanent *now*, despite the occasional references to a period in Chinese history a long time ago. The people who have occasion to use the *I Ching* are chiefly preoccupied with the future. A future that unlike the past presents numerous constantly narrowing options as well as the likelihood of obstacles that may prevent one from proceeding along a path one had hoped to take. The obstacles, incidentally, are all somewhat cryptically depicted in the *I Ching*. One can gather from Wilhelm's introduction to his book *Change*[2] that the German-speaking audience that attended his eight lectures in Peking, by keeping themselves apart from the city's pro-Axis German community, must have faced similar obstacles and danger. It is therefore not too difficult to conjecture what questions Wilhelm might have been asked during and following each lecture. I can see the heavy German faces and brains that are stocked with recollections of Meissen chinaware, Dürer-like landscapes, and damask drapes, ponderously turning to the ancient Chinese text, a text that was able to magnify the elements of chance so alien to the interior of their European apartments in which even the arrangement of the furniture acknowledges an awareness of causality.

Although he may not give it much thought, Cartier-Bresson

[2] Hellmut Wilhelm, *Change: Eight Lectures on the I Ching*, trans. Cary F. Baynes (Princeton, N.J.: Princeton University Press, 1960).

only documents the past. He photographs a eunuch at the Imperial Palace and creates a kind of overlay, one past over another. Yet, looking through his viewfinder Cartier was viewing the present. One might even say that he was selecting from among many an appropriate moment, and then still in the present, not the past, at perhaps one hundredth of a second he transfers the image of that precise moment onto film. What he, quite spontaneously, had framed in his viewfinder turns out to be a wizen-faced eunuch who had served under the Empress Tseu-hi. The eunuch holding some bank notes in one hand is engaged in a conversation with a bald-headed younger man. Quite possibly the eunuch is about to pay the man for some service rendered, or perhaps he has just received the money from the other. By the time Cartier-Bresson gets to examine the print the conversation between the eunuch and the other man belongs to the past. True, they belong to the recent past, but the division between the recent and distant past is somewhat arbitrary. In any case, Cartier's photograph encompasses both, as each shot transcends the immediacy of the situation depicted on the photograph, compelling the viewer to glide from one past to another.

Critically I examine several photographs taken of me, quite vehemently objecting to a few. Why? Because they displease me. I do not care for the image I am projecting. At about the time Wilhelm was delivering his now famous eight lectures on the *Book of Changes* in Peking I was unsuccessfully trying to join the soccer team in my class. I never made it. But, then, as if things were not bad enough, none of my close friends were on the team. This, to my distress, further accentuated the split between the team members and myself. Unlike my friends I was an indifferent student. I was also somewhat of an oddity, failing to fall readily into any of the categories that most groups seem to form at their inception. I recall feeling astonished and somewhat flattered that I could be considered a threat when the mother of a friend of mine showed up at our apartment one day, asking my mother in an icy voice to keep me away from her son since my friendship was having a detrimental effect on his grades. Although my mother made no attempt to enforce this request, my friend and I stopped seeing each other. I don't recall if his grades improved.

At least twice weekly I would accompany my mother to one of

the cafés where she would meet with her acquaintances. Frequently I was the only child at the table. The conversation, held in German, was generally lively and interesting. Everything around us seemed a million miles removed from China. Even the waiters were Austrian or German. I felt extremely pleased with myself whenever I could hold the attention of the grownups with what I considered to be a rather clever remark. From this alone I am led to suspect that I was a rather unpleasant child. In general my statements were made for the benefit of Professor Tonn and whomever else I considered worthy of my interest. Professor Tonn was one of the few people in our community who spoke an excellent Chinese, and had formed a deep interest in Chinese drama and literature. I believe he came to the café because he liked being in the company of so many attentive as well as attractive women. China as a subject, as far as I can remember, was rarely touched upon. My presence, odious as it must have been, was part of the price he had to pay.

In April or May of 1944, a period bracketed by the lectures of Wilhelm and the arrival of Cartier-Bresson in China, Shanghai was bombed sporadically by about a dozen or so B-19s at a time. On one mission they completely missed the Japanese radio station they were trying to destroy, obliterating instead a nearby Chinese market that was crowded with people at that time of day. The following morning a friend and I, drawn as if by a powerful magnet to the totally destroyed area, managed to slip through the barbed-wire barricades that had been set up to prevent all unauthorized people from entering the area. No one paid us the slightest attention as we started out at a rapid pace along the gutted houses and past the occasional body that had not yet been picked up. Everything was still smoldering, and the smell of burnt wood and burnt bodies became thicker the further we walked. We kept on, slightly dazed by now, not knowing where we were going, until we reached a completely deserted square where the dead dismembered bodies had been almost neatly piled up in four or five tall heaps. Seeing the bodies, my friend panicked . . . Before I could stop him he had turned and was running away in the direction we had come. I called out to him, but he didn't stop. Handkerchief pressed to my nose I crossed the square passing between the piles of bodies. For some reason I cannot explain almost anything that lay ahead seemed preferable to taking the same path back. Ten or fifteen minutes later I was able to remove my handkerchief and breathe normally again. When we met the following day I never once mentioned what had happened the day before, but as far as I was concerned, he had left me in the lurch.

I wonder, would Cartier-Bresson have photographed those pyramids of mangled Chinese bodies. Would Wilhelm, had he been in my place, see six thousand years of uninterrupted Chinese history shape a stoic acceptance of chance which, in this particular instant, connected the bomb loads of a dozen B-19s with this sector of Shanghai.

Everything I am able to remember about China, the tattered-looking army of Chiang entering the city, the Chinese brothels, the dance halls, The Little Club packed with American sailors, the Boy Scout Jamboree I faithfully attended, playing Bingo at the racecourse, or the coolies hauling sacks of rice on the Bund, becomes more convincing after I look at Cartier's photographs, whereas the *I Ching* enables me to enter a China I never experienced or saw during my stay there. It is a China devoid of the explicit misery in the shape of dead infants on the sidewalk neatly wrapped in newspaper that I used to pass on my way to school. Yet nothing I have experienced in Shanghai could be said to be foreign to the *I Ching* . . . not even the two Chinese policemen who were playing football with an infant wrapped in newspaper.

How did I respond?

The two policemen were laughing uproariously as they kicked the bundle back and forth across the street. It may have temporarily alleviated their sense of helplessness.

Among my possessions when we left China was a silver cigarette case, a heavy silver ring, and a quite lethal knife. I am still somewhat puzzled by these objects. What did they mean to me? By that time I knew everything the *I Ching* could possibly convey regarding the meeting of two minds. Dwight Irving Gregg, whom I greatly liked and admired inexplicably, aimed his new air gun at me from the first floor balcony of his room. I kept on walking and was hit in the chest. This gratuitous incident, no matter how hard we tried to efface it, signaled the end of our friendship. I, on the other hand, bloodied the nose of an extremely loyal and devoted friend, Herbert Baron. This had all come about shortly after I changed high schools, and Herbert, in order to remain together with me, had persuaded his parents to permit him to do so as well. We both had returned on the school bus from the new school when I on some pretext started to fight with him. It was the only time we had ever fought, and the only time that I had seen Herbert have to defend himself. I started the fight because I was becoming increasingly annoyed by his constant attention. I started the fight because I had several new friends. To make matters worse, I beat him up in front of my new classmates. It was probably the most contemptible thing I had ever done. He left school the following day. I fully realized the implication of my behavior, and so did he. Yet, when we met a year or two later he did not show the slightest hostility. Both our families were intending to leave China. We shook hands before we parted, having carefully avoided the subject of our former friendship. We spoke only of the future. Herbert had never returned to school. More than ever before I was able to realize how low I was able to stoop in order to gain an acceptance that I valued more for the sake of its form than its content. Perhaps this can be disputed, since frequently form and content are inextricably tied together.

During the last few days in Shanghai I rarely ventured out, having narrowly escaped being beaten by a gang of Chinese youths . . . a gang, I might add, that in no way resembled the tattered army of Chiang that I had watched enter the city. I was not taking any chances. China was rapidly losing its allure. It was becoming less and less familiar each day.

From deep inland Cartier-Bresson was heading back to Shanghai, covering the advance of Mao's army and the retreat of the Nationalists. At some time, I feel convinced, our paths must have crossed. I wonder what happened to the eunuch in Cartier's photograph. He and his fellow compatriots must have taken everything in their stride. Since the Ming dynasty the eunuchs have made themselves indispensable to the rulers of Imperial China. At one time these men without balls wielded considerable power and for all practical purpose ran ancient China. Who knows, it could happen again.[3]

---

[3] I realize that the term *without balls* might mislead the reader to infer a weakness where within the context of power none existed. In describing the eunuchs I am simply depicting the potential bureaucratization and corruption of a centralized power such as China today.

Army

In the history of the Sino-Japanese War (1937–45) compiled by Hsu Long-hsuen and Chang Ming-kai, published by the Ching Wu Publishing Co. in Taipeh, Taiwan, the Republic of China, the city of Shanghai is referred to on a number of occasions. To start with there was the Shanghai incident in 1937, although it is not made clear in the book what the incident was about. The book, however, not only covers all the military operations but lists the chain of command and with the aid of dozens of maps shows the military strategy of the Nationalists and of the Japanese forces, who for the most part are simply referred to as the enemy. Charts that show the order of battle during most of the major encounters are also included. Words that most frequently occur are: stopped, combat, readiness, attack, reinforce, mass, advance, reorganize, surprise, intercept, flank, outflank, establish, contact, lose, march, air, cover, shoot, close, combat, gallantly, struggle, fell, back, fought, bitterly, last, man, launch, restore, original, position, lesson, learned, glorious, victory, contribute, immensely, heavy, costly, casualties, capture, main, force, interrupt, enemy, transportation, brigade, garrison, highway, isolated, abandoned, operational, guidance, insure, security, HQ, deployment, shift, disregarding, repelled, halted, feint, attack, broken, suffered, dead, north, south, east, west. The numbers from 1 to 1,000,000 in the book may indicate the number of soldiers, or casualties, or trucks, or pounds of rice, or troops that had successfully escaped encirclement.

Here and there an individual exploit is described, a pleasant break in the seeming repetitiveness of the text. For instance on page 351, beneath the subheading: "Bombing the Enemy Headquarters in Shanghai," there is a brief description of a courageous pilot, Yen Hai-wen, who *by mistake* parachuted into enemy position after his plane was shot down. After killing a number of Japanese soldiers on the ground he committed suicide rather than surrender. Recognizing his gallantry the enemy buried him with full honors and erected a tablet which read, "Tomb of a Gallant Chinese Air Warrior." Even the Japanese press at home covered Yen's gallantry with admiration.

My parents and I arrived in Shanghai several years after this incident. During my stay in Shanghai I remained unaware of a prior conflict in or around the city. Certainly, as far as I was concerned, there was no evidence of it. In the history of the Sino-Japanese War the authors attempt to give a thorough account of how the enemy was gradually worn down and destroyed as he kept advancing and capturing one major Chinese city after the other. It would be simplistic to maintain that the book is merely an attempt at self-deception. Sun Tzu in the *Art of War*, writes: "One yields when it is expedient." By concentrating on the minutiae of the minor skirmishes the authors have managed to avoid touching upon the overwhelming defeat of the Chinese army. In the Orient I believe this is not considered self-deception, it is called saving face. I consider it a major accomplishment if a book is able to achieve that purpose.

In our neighborhood during the war all the air raid wardens were European. A few took their duties with a seriousness that was out of all proportion to what they had to do. My uncle Phoebus's son-in-law, carried away by some inexplicable Germanic zeal, stopped a Japanese army truck during an air raid, claiming that the road was closed to all traffic. When the driver refused to obey, Phoebus's son-in-law lost his temper, and jumping on the running board of the truck, peremptorily ordered the Japanese driver to take him to the local police station. The truck drove off, and my uncle's son-in-law, who in many respects resembled my uncle, was found the next day floating in the Wangpoo River.

After the Japanese surrender the Japanese remained in virtual control of the city until the American and Chinese armies arrived thirteen days later. No attempt was made to attack or molest the Japanese forces in the city. A week after the surrender on my way to a movie I remember seeing a single Japanese soldier standing guard in the center of a large square a short distance from our house. Two hours later when I was on my way home, I found the square packed with Chinese men and women who in an absolute state of frenzy were shouting insults at the soldier. He remained completely still, almost unaffected by the incredible spectacle around him, no trace of any emotion on his broad face. I stood at the edge of the crowd expecting them to attack the soldier, but although they kept inching closer and closer, the attack did not materialize.

My uncle Phoebus, the ex-cavalry man, ex-athlete, could not resist showing his derision toward me, since he—despite my attempts to disguise them—discerned all my flaws, my overwhelming weaknesses. I was never able to win his respect, or prevent him from mimicking my obsessive attachment to games. He did this with a dispassionate but deadly accuracy. For his sake, I am sorry I never became an officer in the Israeli army. It would have made him so happy.

I have in my possession photographs of my uncles Fritz and Phoebus in Austrian uniforms during the First World War. Fritz was killed shortly after his photograph was taken by a certain R. Frantz, Wien XIV, Mariahilferstrasse. Fell on the twenty-fourth of June 1915 in Ruda Koszilua, Poland. Buried beside a windmill next to a brook, it says on the back. I wonder if my uncle Phoebus was able to refrain from mimicking the entry into Shanghai of the *victorious* Nationalist army. At least half the soldiers I saw were under fifteen. A good many were barefoot. Only a most enthusiastic supporter of Chiang could have evinced any pride in the army. To me it was simply one more inexplicable and unexpected spectacle in a world rich with strange and bizarre spectacles. But often it seemed to me that I was the only one who felt that way.

Idea

Under certain conditions ideas tend toward a common goal, toward a sameness of purpose. Deprivation of any sort is generally a good impetus to the formation of an idea that might alter the situation for the better. Inventions of all kinds are predicated on ideas, and quite frequently, when an idea is said to be in the air, people who may be separated by thousands of miles reach the same idea. In order for an idea to be effective it need not be complicated or particularly ingenious. I don't know who first made a replica of a pistol out of soap and then attempted to rob a bank or escape from jail. Making a pistol out of soap is not the easiest thing in the world. A rudimentary knowledge of the weapon is essential. The ingredients for the mock pistol, soap, black shoe polish, are however easily available. It goes without saying that the weapon would be useless in a hot boiler room, or in the proximity of a stove.

Some people who are not in jail are quite capable of thinking up ideas for people who are. Usually, when an idea becomes formalized, that is to say, when it is workable, it is patented. Ideas are also something to share with others. They allow people to create a bond, an impermanent bond perhaps, but all the same, a bond. I have an idea, someone says, and everyone perks up his ears. What will it be? They will share it. Ideas contain privileged information. I have shared some of my ideas with friends. I have a great idea, I said . . .

The inventor is filled with torment. He wishes to reveal his ideas to one and all, but is aware of the danger of doing so. Someone else might carry off the glory, the honor . . . Who really had the idea of inventing the camera, the Morse code, the radio . . .

Who was the first Chinese emperor to use eunuchs as confidential secretaries, emmisaries, and flunkies, knowing that the eunuchs' loyalty would not be subject to the same temptations as that of members of the nobility at court. I unexpectedly won a short-story competition at school and in front of the class was complimented by my teacher for thinking up a story about a story competition in which the winning student had somehow managed to take the other students aside, one by one, and under the guise of friendship given them an idea for a story they could use, but in each case it was the same story. Having won the competition I lived in dread for the remainder of the term, afraid that my teacher or someone else in the class might happen across the *Rover Boys Annual* from which I had lifted the idea. I was aware that my winning the first prize by plagiarizing had added a certain richness to the original story. The only pity was that I could not share the information with anyone.

When I married for the first time it was in a sense the result of an idea to keep H from having to join the Israeli army, which as a married woman she would not have to do. As a result of this idea I went through a somewhat farcical marriage and then, six months later, through an equally farcical divorce. Throughout our marriage I kept maintaining that it was simply a poetic gesture. (This brings to mind a statement by Arrabal that by poet he does not mean one who writes poems, but a terrorist or provocateur, who never writes. I have extremely mixed feelings regarding that statement now.) I kept my marriage a secret from my friends. With the exception of one person, no one knew that I was married. I lived alone and rarely saw my wife, although at one time we had been in love and lived together for a year. On the day of my wedding I had gone to see a writer I greatly admired and confided to him what I was about to do. It was he who later introduced me to Kierkegaard, and it was he who strongly urged me to abandon my idea, saying that he didn't think it to be a very good one. He was extremely tactful.

Real

Language is used chiefly to document what is real. There is no lack of interpretations for everything that takes place or fails to take place in our bedroom, in our living room, in the bathroom, on the stairs, in the street, or in a swamp, but what the interpretations share in common is a concern with the real . . . The history of the Sino-Japanese War strives to be real. For all I know it is totally false, perhaps there never was an airman called Yen who parachuted by mistake into enemy position, and then committed suicide, but in this particular book the incident is made real. The charts, the dates, even the hours of certain battles add to the reality. True, we expect the real to be convincing, but it is almost impossible to verify the battle of Western Hupei where purportedly forty-one enemy planes were downed. Still, all in all, Shanghai is real. It exists. When Dwight Irving Gregg shot at me with his BB gun it was real, yet lacking a proper explanation for his conduct, and never receiving one, I remained puzzled. The reality of our friendship was undermined by an incident I could not explain. A plausible explanation is that he happened to be standing on his balcony, holding a BB gun he had just received for his birthday, when I came along . . .

When a friend whom I had not seen in years called me one day and asked: How are you? I replied that I felt dislocated and unreal. Why did I say that. What made me feel unreal . . . What is the absence of the real . . . Since everything I have ever seen seems tinged with a certain unreality, I can only conclude that unreality is entirely subjective, that in fact the viewer brings or attaches his unreality to what he sees. Wearing a Scout hat, and trying to earn a semaphore badge, I did not feel unreal, attending a Scout's jamboree I did not feel unreal, entering a luxurious Chinese whorehouse at the age of fifteen, and being confronted by a row of immensely attractive women, I felt aware of something less than real. I don't know when precisely, but the message: *Is there any other way to live?* that we may expect to receive any day from outer space carries within it the pathos of the real. From the message one will be able to conclude that the real is a boundary separating us from the hazards of our desires for everything that is new. The *I Ching* it must be stated is not, contrary to what many people believe, an oracular book. It is simply a guide to the real. In Kafka's *Castle* K. the surveyor strives for recognition from the Castle. He endeavors to have the Castle bestow its reality on him . . . and once or twice it does so, acknowledging his presence. Someone at the Castle even states that they (whoever they are) are satisfied with his progress. But this is all the more baffling since as far as he can determine he has made no progress at all.

Daily we are witnesses of the ceremony surrounding the real, or to put it another way, the ceremony of the real. Standing at attention at a parade ground in the former British army camp, Sarafand, I was not a participant of the real, I was an element that enabled the parade to be real. Standing under the canopy at my wedding, my future wife and I were culprits of a fraud . . . We went through all the expected responses and finally were congratulated by a couple of witnesses who had been paid to attend. I permitted the ceremony to intensify the reality of an isolation I wished to experience. The wedding, for me, was equivalent to stepping through the mirror in Cocteau's film *Orpheus*.

Where

I've been to an extraordinary whorehouse, someone said, and I promptly asked: Where is it? The question *where* elicits all kinds of pertinent information. People, in general, are only too glad to divulge *where* they buy their shirts, and *where* they vacation, and *where* one can get a stuffed owl at a decent price. Perfect strangers confide to me *where* they live, *where* they work, *where* they met their husband or wife, as the case may be.

As a young boy in Shanghai I discovered quite by accident a most incredible mazelike building in which actors, jugglers, magicians gave a continuous performance to the people who drifted from one large chamber to another. I soon lost all sense of direction, walking down long corridors, circling one courtyard then another, stopping for a while to buy something to eat, then watching a puppet performance, and a man on stilts, and a peacock chained to a table . . . all the time aware that I was the only non-Chinese in the crowd. I returned a couple of times, always alone. I recall having described the building and what went on inside it to my friends without once eliciting the question: *Where?*

In retrospect this doesn't come as a surprise, since China was largely excluded from our minds. It certainly was excluded from our textbooks at school, since these were the standard English textbooks. I vividly remember the colored maps of Africa and South America, but not the map of China . . . After all, why study China. All one had to do was to take a look out of the window and one could get a pretty good idea what China was like.

Still, Cartier must have asked *where?* when he arrived. Briefly, after school I worked for a former manager of Leitz Optics who repaired Leicas and Rolleis for the foreign correspondents. Once I watched him take apart a Leica that had been dropped in a river during the fighting inland. Could it, I wonder, have belonged to Cartier-Bresson?

When I first met H I had just bought a camera. It was a fairly inexpensive camera made in France. By that time Cartier-Bresson had already taken his photographs of the eunuchs, and the Chinese wedding procession, and numerous shots of the fleeing Nationalist army, and the portrait of a former Chinese warlord, as well as shots of faces, simply curious faces staring at Cartier with his assortment of cameras as he casually and unself-consciously kept stopping on the street, and lifting one of his battered cameras to eye level, snapped their curious stares . . . of course, in a sense, he was intruding, as every single white man who arrived in China intruded . . . but by then these intrusions were taken for granted. Just another foreigner intrigued with their signs, their life-style, their rituals . . .

I took a few photographs of H in a public park in the north of Tel Aviv. Unlike Cartier I was a bit self-conscious and kept fumbling with the camera as I calculated the f opening and the shutter speed . . . H smiled, but because of the prolonged wait, the smile became somewhat strained. It wasn't spontaneous anymore when I snapped the picture, it was strained the way it would be later at our wedding.

How comforting and reassuring it is to find a map attached to a wall upon which an arrow has been drawn pointing to where on the map one happens to be. You are here, it says beneath the arrow as I calculate the distance and the time that separates me from my destination.

EIGHT POEMS

JAIME GIL DE BIEDMA

Translated from the Spanish by Louis M. Bourne

TRANSLATOR'S NOTE. *In an essay on Luis Cernuda, one of the major Spanish poets of the "Generation of '27," Jaime Gil de Biedma writes that "the fundamental experience of living is in the ambivalence of identity," the conflicting awareness of oneself as child of god and child of one's social environment. His own poems stem from his consciousness of the uneasy relationship between himself and his double, the loving or treacherous persona of his word, or between himself and his neighbor. While his poetry is based on a simulacrum of real experience and, above all, on the growing awareness of the personal meaning of events, its implications frequently tend to be ironic. Life, while compelling the poet to gather sensations, leads him through a dialectic of nostalgia and disillusion. His poems about love deal with its disquieting aftermath, and his "social" po-etry, when not directly critical of the pervading gloom of post-Civil War Spanish society, forms either a sardonic commentary on his own pleasures or an indictment of the existential "bad faith" of his bourgeois background.*

Born in Barcelona in 1929, Gil de Biedma continues to live and work there in a tobacco company. The Civil War years he spent in Nava de la Asunción, a village in the province of Segovia, where he still summers. He studied law at the University of Barcelona.

His first book of poems, Según sentencia del tiempo ("According to the Sentence of Time") *appeared in 1953. This was followed by* Compañeros de viaje ("Traveling Companions," *1959*), Moralidades ("Moralities," *1966*), *and* Poemas póstumos ("Posthumous Poems," *1968*). Cuatro poemas morales ("Four Moral Poems," *1965*) *was a preview of "Moralities";* En favor de Venus ("In Favor of Venus," *1965*) *was later divided among his last three books. His first collected poems,* Colección particular ("Private Collection," *1969*) *was banned by the censor, though it finally came out in an expanded form,* Las personas del verbo ("The Personas of the Word"), *in 1975. As a critic, Gil de Biedma has published a work on* Cántico: el mundo y la poesía de Jorge Guillén ("Canticle: The World and Poetry of Jorge Guillén," *1960*). *He has translated Eliot's* The Use of Poetry and the Use of Criticism *and Christopher Isherwood's* Goodbye to Berlin *into Spanish. In 1974, his* Diario del artista seriamente enfermo ("Diary of an Artist Seriously Ill") *appeared.*

The modern poem begins for Jaime Gil de Biedma with the secularization of society, as the middle class became consolidated at the time of the Romantic movement, a change he finds reflected in Byron's Don Juan. *Like Yvor Winters, whom he quotes in* Moralities, *Gil de Biedma's artistic process is to bring the pressure of reason to bear on his feelings in order to evaluate morally his experience and determine the kind and intensity of its emotion.*

ANNIVERSARY WALTZ

There is nothing so sweet as a room
For two, when we don't love each other now too much,
Away from the city, in a peaceful hotel,
And doubtful couples and some child with ganglions,

If it is not this slight sensation
Of unreality. Something like summer
At my parents' house some years ago,
Like train trips at night. I call to you

To say that I am not saying anything
That you don't already know, or maybe
To kiss you vaguely
On the same lips.

You have come in from the balcony.
The room has grown dark
While we look at each other tenderly, uneasy
At not feeling the weight of three years.

Everything is the same, it seems
As though it weren't yesterday. And this nostalgic taste
That the silences put in our mouths
Possibly leads us to be mistaken

About our feelings. But not
Without some reserve, because underneath
Something is pulling more strongly and it is (to say it
Perhaps in a less imprecise way)

Difficult to remember that we love each other,
If it is not with a certain vagueness, and Saturday,
Which is today, remains so close
To yesterday at the last moment and to the day after

Tomorrow
In the morning . . .

CHILDHOOD AND CONFESSIONS

for Juan Goytisolo

When I was younger
(Well, really, better to say
Very young)
              some years before

Knowing you and
Recently arrived in the city,
I often thought about life.
                              My family
Was quite rich and I, a student.

My childhood was memories of a house
With a school and a cupboard and key in the closet,
Of when the comfortable
Families,
          as the term implies,
Summered endlessly
At Stephanie Villa or at Belvedere
Mansion
          and the world beyond continued on
With gravel paths and rustic
Summerhouses, decorated with pompous hydrangeas,
All slightly egotistical and out-of-date.
I was born (pardon me)
In the age of the pergola and tennis.

Life, however, had strange limits
And what is stranger still: a certain tendency
To withdraw.
               Painful stories were told,
Unexplained happenings,
Nobody knew where, sad faces,
Basements cold as churches.
                              Something muffled
Endured far off
And it was possible, they said at home,
To go blind from a scare.

From my fortunate little kingdom,
This habit of warmth remains
And an impossible penchant for myth.

THE GHOSTS

It was this very morning,
In the middle of the street.

                          I was waiting
With the others, beside the traffic light,
And suddenly I felt a slight rub,
Almost like a tugging at my sleeve.
                                Then,
As I hurried across,
The vision of some terrible eyes blew in
From who-knows-what painful void.

It just happens that this occurs
Too often.
             And yet,
At least in some of us,
A wake of hidden anxiety remains,
A certain feeling of guilt.
                          I remember,
Too, on a beautiful afternoon
When I was going back home . . . A woman
Collapsed at my side, folded up
On herself; quietly
And with an unbelievable slowness—I held her
By the armpits, for a moment, the face,
An old one, almost glued to mine.
Then, without coming to yet,
She raised her eyes where nothing
Could be read but the pure want
That gave me thanks.
                    I turned around
To see her going painfully down the street.

I don't know how to explain it; it's
As if everything,
As if the world around me
Had stopped
But cynically continued
To move, as

If nothing, as if nothing were true.
No ghost
That goes by, no body in pain,
Foreshadows death; each one says death was
Already among us without our knowing.

                                  They come
From there, from the other side of the sulfurous depths,
From the silent
Mines of hunger and crowds.
And they don't even know who they are:
The living dead.

FEAR COMES ON

Fear comes on with a stagnant
Swell. Suddenly, here,
It creeps in:
The known structures, the possible

Consequences foreseen (which don't exclude
The worst),
All the slow mastery of the intelligence
And its limited alternatives, everything

Goes blank in an instant.
And only the root remains,
Something like a painful antenna,
Limp, one doesn't know why, throbbing.

ASTURIAS, 1962

Just as after an explosion
The silence changes, so the war

Left us deafened for a long time.
And each strict individual life
Was to shriek against the wall
Of a thick silence made of newspaper.

Gray years stubbornly
Spent learning how not to feel deaf,
Nor any more lonely than what it is human
For men to be . . . But today
The silence is different, because it is charged.
Confidence has come back to visit us,

While we imagine a landscape
Of coalbins at the mine entrances
And of motionless cranes, like a snapshot.

PEEPING TOM

Eyes of a loner, bewildered boy
Whom I surprised staring at us
In that pine grove beside the Faculty of Arts
More than eleven years ago,

When I started to pull myself away,
Still stunned with sand and saliva,
After we rolled around, the two of us half dressed,
Blissful as beasts.

Your memory, how strange,
With the condensed strength of a symbol,
Stays linked to that story,
My first experience of requited love.

At times I ask myself what happened to you.
And if now, in your nights next to a body,
The old scene returns
And you still spy our kisses.

So the image of your eyes
Returns to me from the past
Like an unrelated scream. Expression
Of my own desire.

AGAINST JAIME GIL DE BIEDMA

What good is it, I must know, to change apartments,
To leave behind a basement blacker
Than my reputation—and that's saying something—,
To put up white curtains
And take on a maid,
Give up the bohemian life,
If later you come, bore,
Embarrassing guest, idiot dressed up in my clothes,
Drone of the beehive, useless fool,
With your scrubbed hands,
To eat from my plate and dirty my house?

The counters of the last bars
Of the night accompany you, the pimps, the flower ladies,
The dead streets of dawn
And the elevators with their yellow lights,
When you arrive, drunk,
And you stop to see your destroyed face
In the mirror,
With still violent eyes
That you don't want to close. And if I rebuke you,
You laugh, you remind me about the past
And say I am growing old.

I could remind you that now you have no charm.
That your casual style and nonchalance
Turn out to be downright awful
When you are older than thirty,
And that your charming
Lazy, boyish smile—

So sure to please—is a painful residue,
A pathetic attempt.
While you look at me with your true
Orphan's eyes, and you cry for me
And promise me you won't do it again.

If you weren't such a bitch!
And if only I didn't know, for a while now,
That you are strong when I am weak
And you are weak when I get furious . . .
Of your returns, I still retain a confused impression
Of panic, of sorrow and unhappiness,
And the despair
And the impatience and the resentment
Of suffering again, once more,
The unforgivable humiliation
Of too much intimacy.

With effort, I shall haul you off to bed,
Like somebody who is going to hell
To sleep with you.
Dying from impotence at every step,
Tripping over furniture,
Groping, we shall cross the apartment,
Awkwardly embracing, reeling
With alcohol and repressed sobs.
Oh mean bondage to love human beings,
And meanest of all
Is to love yourself!

DE VITA BEATA

In an old inefficient country,
Something like Spain between two
Civil wars, in a village by the sea,
To own a house and a small income
And no memory. Not to read,
Not to suffer, not to write, not to pay bills,
And to live like a ruined noble
Among the ruins of my intelligence.

FOUR COLLAGES

HOWARD STERN

The Big Orange.

Concrete Poster II

Listen to those dancing feet!

Don't listen to those dancing feet!

THE CHAPLINIAD

A Film Poem

IVAN GOLL

Translated from the German by Frank Jones

I

Chaplin comes to life on one of the thousand posters than adorn the city. He gazes in wonder at the people passing in the street, steps down carefully from the pedestal on which he had been pictured as the King of Hearts, and gravely deposits crown, scepter, orb in an ashcan.

CHAPLIN: The kings and I have been posters long enough—
Always smiling, rain or shine,
Grinning at the everlasting moment!
I want to be myself,
Able to weep when suffering:
I want to get a summer haircut
And forget all about the police.

A billposter crosses the street at an angle and starts putting up a perfume advertisement. Chaplin, who has slipped behind the pillar, soon reappears in his usual garb: bowler hat, short jacket, small cane, baggy pants. The billposter swears and gesticulates furiously.

BILLPOSTER: Hey, Chaplin, what's the big idea?

Back to your poster, fool!
Work! Smile! That's your profession!
Chaplin pokes around thoughtfully in the ashcan, picks up with his cane the crown he had laid aside.
CHAPLIN: I give the crown to you: let me go free.
I pity the bored unhappy passer-by,
I was glad to beautify those gray streets of his,
But I tell you it's getting harder
To live for one alone than to die for all mankind.
BILLPOSTER (*slaps Chaplin in the face*):
Wisdom comes easy with five million a year.
As for me, I'm a socialist.
To every man his morals and his raincoat!
Pedestrians start walking around the poster pillar in a grotesque procession, as if searching for something, and utter generalities in a bored way as if reciting lessons.
TUTOR: Dig no grave for others and you'll fall in yourself.
JOURNALIST: The early bird gets the coffee.
LIEUTENANT: I think it's raining.
LADY: It's not raining.
TUTOR: It's raining a bit.
OLDER GENTLEMAN: It's coming on to rain.
LIEUTENANT: It's pouring.
BILLPOSTER (*furiously*): Onto the poster, wretch!
CHAPLIN: Tragic the fool, mimicking folly,
Tragic the acrobat, facing death for smiles;
They are the loneliest in the world—
And woe to them if they are recognized!
The crowd does not forgive the lonely ones
Their solitude.
The billposter seizes Chaplin by the collar and pushes him toward the pillar. Chaplin appears for a moment as Christ crowned with thorns. But the billposter implacably sticks him back on the pillar.
Now Chaplin stands aloft, life-size.
The pedestrians greet him. A smile on every face. A dismal-looking hunchback comes by. Chaplin is frightened, then grows very sad, then: bursts out laughing, shows his gleaming teeth, holds his belly, laughs till the hunchback laughs too. Now Chaplin turns and secretly wipes a tear.

Somebody gives the billposter a tip. Delighted, he claps a hand to his brow, then stands close in front of Chaplin, holding out his cap to the crowd like a beggar.

A group of boys appear, growing very hot as they leapfrog around the pillar. They laugh. Chaplin cheers up. (Chaplin is only the mirror of all the world). Shown on screen: LET THE LITTLE CHILDREN COME TO ME . . . And Chaplin steps onto the billposter's head, leaps free of his poster, and leapfrogs the last boy in the line.

The billposter falls headlong. His money spills in the gutter. Chaplin runs off. All pedestrians after him: flight through the streets. A chase along boulevards, in buses, through restaurants, apartments, subway stations. The pursuers, grasping at a vanished happiness, grow even more numerous. But suddenly all Chaplin posters break loose from pillars, buildings, construction fences: Chaplin in every conceivable costume—as dishwasher, soldier, king, clerk, violin virtuoso, all gather so that soon the pursued outnumber the pursuers. The crowd are at a loss whom to chase. The instant they seize a Chaplin he falls, limp as a paper poster. And the Chaplins of the earth gradually increase, then abruptly turn, become One, the living Chaplin. He laughs. Universal laughter and embraces. (Symbolic victory of the good genius over the poor in spirit).

Chaplin stands alone. His brow clears.

CHAPLIN: A longing for the human makes us greater.
The silence is one that cannot be matched.
The world moves gently now:
You hold the globe in balance on your finger
And hurl it back into infinity!

II

An express train comes by. Chaplin springs into an empty compartment which contains a library and a table with a variety of writing implements.

At regular intervals he leans out of the window to study the scenery through the big binoculars. Abruptly he leans back and writes:

To be inspired: is that to be unthinking?
We expect the waves of sunset to strike us from without,
Blocks of marble are supposed to pile up into a Doric temple,
My mind has been switched off.

Chaplin looks out again through the glasses. Glorious Alpine landscape. Jagged peaks. A herd of chamois on a glacial slope.
I was more excited when pink postcards brought me
The elegy of the Matterhorn in my home town in fall.
That was true elevation:
The alpenglow of longing and of life
Brought by the postman
Made me a poet from that moment on!
The binoculars shift. Bare railroad embankment. Telegraph poles loom up, whiz by. A stationmaster's pleasant house, with tulips around it and an elderberry bush. Film still.
Little everyday landscape! I find you divine.
Grass, how noble! Bellflowers tell the wind:
"Wait two thousand years and you will love me more."
To live is to grow old;
Death rejuvenates.
He puts down the binoculars. Very sad. Suddenly he picks up the fountain pen. New landscape: meadow. Brown herds. Gnarled willow trunks.
Little calf, tender in the cosmic clover,
How sad your mystic gaze!
You know as much as I of the world's pain.
The train stops. A lady enters the compartment with a deer on a silken leash. Chaplin moves into a corner.
Someone has robbed me of my solitude!
Contact with metaphysical space is interrupted.
On such a day as this mankind invented fate.
LADY (*smiles*): Have you a round-trip ticket to Elysium too?
My brother-in-law wants to build a chemical dye plant there.
I've talked him out of it because of the poor connections.
CHAPLIN: You're not intending suicide, I hope?
LADY: That too, perhaps. What else can one do to be interesting?
My daughter Dearie is weak on her little china legs.
Whenever a gentleman greets us she collapses—
Spring and the glow of evening don't pay any more.
Men understood nothing about us women.
CHAPLIN: I want to carry your daughter in my arms all over the
    world,
I want to give her my writings to nibble every day;

All my poems
Inscribed with swallows:
Poets should write only for deer,
Verses belong in the woods where they began!

LADY: You're the quiet kind. I'd love to travel with you.
I have antique memories of Parnassus.
Have you a checkbook?

CHAPLIN (*searching*): The Book of Ruth I have. But a check-book . . .

LADY (*throwing her arms round his neck*):
What will you write in it for me? Ten thousand?

THE DEER: Shall I turn round now, Mama?

LADY (*to Chaplin*): Shall we stop at the Hotel Zeus or the
    Terminus?

CHAPLIN (*desperate*): Wherever you please—but separate
    showers!

(*Looking out the window.*) Wasn't I going to Nature? The pine
    trees' shade?
To watch the rivers flow into the sea?
Madam, I beg of you, don't love me.
Let me be lonely, beating my head on the stones in comfortless
    grief:
Do me a favor: don't love me! It's so tiring!

*Chaplin takes his cane off the hook and stabs the lady in the
heart. She falls dead.*

THE DEER: Shall I cry now, Mama?

*Chaplin hugs the deer, strokes it. He stuffs the lady's corpse under
the seat. The train stops. He leaps out nimbly with the deer.*

III

*Chaplin enters the station restaurant. No customers. In a corner the
stationmaster, whose wife manages the restaurant, is seated with his
family at their midday meal.*

*Chaplin puts on a sad look, walks back and forth faster and
faster: a hunger dance. He climbs up and down the walls, then
mounts the stationmaster's table and marches among the dishes. The
family feasts on without a break.*

WIFE: Cripes, it's Charlie!

You look pale, like everyone who takes this road.
Behind the house lies Parnassus Graveyard,
Planted with pink laurels;
There rest all poets who looked tired like you.

The stationmaster gives his spouse a furious look, stamps on her slippers under the table. Chaplin shakes his head in refusal but sits down at the table, ties a napkin round a knee, brandishes knife and fork. The stationmaster puts a slice of bread on Chaplin's plate, meanwhile halving a roast chicken and serving himself and his wife.

WIFE: Living is so expensive! Potatoes are so expensive! Won't you have dinner with us?

Chaplin pushes the bread around his plate, holds it up to the light, takes a postal scale from his pocket, weighs the bread on it.

CHAPLIN: Couldn't you give me a rose petal?

STATIONMASTER (*to wife*): Give him one from the dead rose in the vase.

Wife gets up, takes the bread off Chaplin's plate, pulls a rose to pieces in its place.

WIFE: And how bread's gone up!

An entire cauliflower is sliced and divided between husband and wife.

CHAPLIN: The inside of this rose is too much for my wolfish hunger.

STATIONMASTER: Yes, a man must watch his waistline. Once you get hungry, that is, become an idealist . . .

At this point the deer jumps in by the window, knocks the table over, and takes shelter with Chaplin. Uproar in the house. But Chaplin walks to the window with the animal, pulls out a piece of paper, contemplates the evening, and writes (script on screen):

Whoever looks at this pink cloud with me,
This calm event
In the dying evening,
If just one among the million greets it,
From waiting room, ticket window, boulevard—
That one is my friend.

Chaplin folds the paper; the deer gobbles it.

A train is announced. The stationmaster rushes out. His wife sets the signals.

During this interval Chaplin hurries to the buffet table and devours everything in sight—cutlets, sausages, oranges; pours a bottleful of brandy on his hair; washes his hands in champagne.

Then both dash out. Uproar. Pursuit.

Chaplin strolls with his cane along the tops of the train cars, smoking a cigar. He multiplies himself by two, by ten: his pursuers become confused. All this at high speed. At last Chaplin sits down on the locomotive, facing backward, and rides away on the modern Pegasus with the deer.

CHAPLIN: Parnassus, deserted by birds and treetops,
You are a clay-pile of ancient centuries!
Express, tell me the land of purity!
Perhaps the girls are faithful in Japan?
Perhaps I have a friend in the Hawaiian Isles?
The last god lives in Greenland?
Poor me, poor Chaplin! If I had a homeland
Any place would be home for me.
But is there ever peace and quiet for a poet?

IV

Chaplin wanders in the desert, pulling the deer on a rope. He sits down on a dune after spreading his handkerchief and kissing the ground Bedouin style.

CHAPLIN: Whoever beats his head against the wall in anguish
    understands me.
Whoever insanely awaits the impossible beloved day after day
    in subway stations understands me.
Whoever is revolted by hotel beds, whoever suffocates in living
    rooms,
Come you all to my prophetic heart
And weep three springs into the desert with me.
That is the only possible kindness.

    He absent-mindedly tips his hat.
How many suicidal actions I've committed!
Tonight millions are laughing at my follies:
Now I may mourn at last.
Charlie of Assisi!
You know about suffering, timid deer, as I do.
Miserable creature, always hungry!

(*Yawning*) How lovely it is here, and quiet (*yawning*) at God's
    feet!
The sky is constantly the same,
My shadow creeps in boredom at my side.
Europe is so far! Straight down below us
A purple city lies.
How I long, how I long for it!
    *He begins to dig. The earth opens. Fantastic views of the earth's
interior. On reaching its center Chaplin puts a telephone receiver to
his ear and listens, as at the center of a telephone system, to the
voices of all the world (heard as from a phonograph):*
    *Ten million butterflies / Elderly baker murdered / Un jour
viendra / In the year 800 Charlemagne was / All or nothing, I say /
112-degree fever / Macaroni with red tomatoes / I love the lady
from Zanzibar / Bitte schön / Christson & Co., collars and men's
wash / Shuttle train to Marathon / The radicals are frightened / Là
là là petite femme / No, better yesterday than tomorrow / Charlot-
tenburg 6 / Brains baked in butter . . .*
    CHAPLIN: Is that all anybody thinks of?
A roaring at the center of the earth:
Tumult of lies, telephoned stupidity, craziness of radiograms.
What a poor thing is man! All literatures melt away
At the golden word: pain!
The fountainhead of brains sparkles with numbers
And empty bubbles sink from starry skies
To burst in the waters of canals.
Graveyards weigh all memory down with heavy stones:
We all love wrongly always.
Only the longing
For endless illusion is true:
Truth makes us yawn.
    *Suddenly: the port of Marseilles. Frenzied traffic: streetcars, heavy
trucks, people of all races. Shouting. A news vendor yells in Chap-
lin's ear: RED HEART, THE SOCIALIST DAILY! Chaplin doffs
his hat and makes the man a low, earnest bow. This upsets him.
Chaplin strolls along the streets, smugly twirling his cane.*
    *Gradually he becomes aware of the new European social order.
Everyone works. Scorn is poured on anyone thinking at leisure.
Thin, bespectacled intellectuals crush paving stones in cadence.*

Women climb roofs and let down ropes. Men in top hats drive streetcars. Children help parents at their work. Beside each person stands a guard with a gas mask and a fixed bayonet. On street corners where once stood the words PRESERVE THE ANIMALS! we read in thick letters (script on screen) PRESERVE YOUR BRAINS! JOIN THE THINKERS' UNION!

The vendor annoyed by Charlie's greeting chases him with a large uniformed troop. Chaplin eludes his attackers by the power of his thinking: we glimpse him now in a Cairo square, now on a street in Hong Kong.

Then the same street in Marseilles.

From its other side a new crowd approaches, carrying a placard: INTELLECTUAL WANTED! SALARY IN MILLIONS! The leader of this crowd rushes up to Chaplin and falls at his knees.

LEADER: Hail Charlie!

Hail, liberator from the age of toil!

Lead us back to ourselves!

Strange brother of the deer, prophet of desert peoples,

We languish here and thirst for your art:

Strike the stony fountain of our breast!

Grant mankind the gift of laughter,

Make heaven flow into our eyes again!

We can't think any more,

We recognize ourselves no longer!

Redeem us from work! Bring on the communism of the soul!

CHAPLIN: And the pay in millions?

LEADER: Not one, ten million hearts are at your service.

Free mankind from boredom!

Bring us the revolution!

Deeply moved, Chaplin looks at him, steps back, and wipes his tie and vest with his handkerchief.

CHAPLIN (*in an undertone*): Could you please move aside a little?

You keep spitting on me.

The crowd, believing Chaplin has said something important to their leader, rejoices; he is surrounded and hoisted to the top of a halted streetcar.

Thus elevated he waves his hat at people, flicks dust from a sleeve, looks all ways, smiles, waves.

The excited crowd pushes forward, shouts, pulls him back down, carries him off in triumph.

New encounter with the news vendor and his countless cops. Fracas. Battle. The armed men win; people flee. Chaplin, left alone in the streets, takes an ocarina from his vest pocket, sits down on the sidewalk, and plays a tune. His eyes brighten. His brow high, serious.

The street quite empty. Suddenly a harmless lone policeman appears in the background. Chaplin looks up, gets scared, throws the flute away and runs off as fast as his heels will carry him, narrowing to a pinpoint in the fadeout.

V

Chaplin strolls in a dark wood. Tall pines. Blackberry bushes. Sunflower-sized violets. Birds fly round and round his hat. A botanist's box hangs from his shoulder.

The deer trips along beside him, a pink ribbon round its neck.

Chaplin stops from time to time and looks at it with feeling. Then he opens the box and takes out a verse machine. After a lengthy reverie he taps on a birch trunk. (Script on screen)

CHAPLIN: All birds have twittered
Out of spring—
All blond streams
Flow from God's heart—
What is the world, my love?
Just an illusion
Made up by both of us!

The deer is transformed into a young girl.

DEARIE: Enough playing deer and acting poetic!
Enough fake sentiment!
Longing only causes tuberculosis.

CHAPLIN: I used to believe in dreams
But even the nymphs have turned bourgeois.

DEARIE: Have we had our fill of stars?
Are we respected for benevolence?
The whole world laughs at you.
You're a wretched hypochondriac
And a rotten match!
I don't love you any more! I don't love you any more!

At the back of the wood appears a red boar, a bearded hunter, a dog. At once Dearie runs off, flings her arms round the man's neck. They vanish together.

Chaplin grasps the pink ribbon with which he had been leading the deer, looks around, slowly prepares to hang himself from the birch. Comic interludes. At the last moment a squirrel chews through the ribbon. Chaplin comes to a pond, takes off his shoes, puts them on again. He tries the water, finally wades in up to his knees. Finds it too cold. In the wood, Dearie runs away from the hunter. Chaplin tries to rush to her aid. The hunter fires. She falls, dying.

CHAPLIN: Now I'm more miserable than on the first day.
My fate pours down on me like rain,
My heart's as stiff as a dead clock.
That's Chaplin!
Lonelier than anyone!
Europe laughs, New York and every village laughs
And won't believe how deeply I suffer,
And one—the little mother behind the curtain
Who waited more than twenty years
For a letter from Charlie,
The only woman who's never been to the movies—
If she saw me sobbing
She'd laugh too!

For some time all the posters have been creeping in, as in the opening scene. They bow low to Chaplin. The billposter grabs him and pastes him back on the pillar.

SONG FOR THAT MAN OF THE PEOPLE, CHARLIE CHAPLIN

CARLOS DRUMMOND DE ANDRADE

Translated from the Brazilian Portuguese and introduced by Giovanni Pontiero

CARLOS DRUMMOND DE ANDRADE'S ODE TO CHARLIE CHAPLIN

Giovanni Pontiero

Carlos Drummond de Andrade, who is now in his late seventies, has won universal esteem as Brazil's major contemporary poet. He was born on October 31, 1902, in Itabira in the state of Minas Gerais and has enjoyed a long, prolific, and distinguished career as poet, journalist, critic, and essayist.

His first experiments with verse coincided with the emergence of the Modernist movement in Brazil in the early twenties. As a prominent contributor to the short-lived Modernist journal *A Revista* (*"The Review"*), which he helped to launch in 1925, Drummond de Andrade was able to clarify his own constructive role within the plethora of literary debates and theories which were aired during those stormy years. The aesthetics which have come to characterize the poet's wholly personal voice were already evident in his first book of verse, *Alguma Poesia* (*"Some Poetry"*) published in 1930. The poems of this early collection are composed in clear straightforward language which often assumes a colloquial note. The poet specializes in simple annotations and wry asides as he reflects upon the external world without indulging in any literary preconceptions or affectation. In mood, he favors a subtle interplay between stoic detachment and deep emotional involvement as he comes face to face with the "enormous reality" of Man's universe, hovering as it does between the tragic and the absurd.

The most striking of Drummond de Andrade's poems capture life as the poet knows it to be—comfortingly humdrum and familiar yet ever capable of unexpected reversals. The human experiences he probes strike every chord from zany humor to the most bitter pathos, from things sublime to moments of sheer banality. The poems tend to become more penetrating and somber as Drummond de Andrade progresses into a more mature phase with such key collections of verse as *Sentimento do Mundo* ("*Sentiment of the World*"), which appeared in 1940, and *A Rosa do Povo* ("*The Rose of the People*"), published five years later in 1945. A renewed sense of urgency takes possession of the poet when he meditates upon the horrors of the Second World War and its legacy of hatred and strife. Innocence, love, and serenity symbolized by floral gardens and childhood games seem irretrievable as dark shadows engulf the world and politicians and industrialists gamble away the common man's right to live in freedom and security. And who is more apt to represent the anonymous man buffeted by the whims of the rich and mighty than that legendary screen-image, the late Charlie Chaplin, whom more than one critic defined as "the most universal being of our time" and whom George Bernard Shaw acclaimed as "the only genius ever developed in motion pictures"?

When Chaplin received the Stalin Peace Prize, he declared: "I am a citizen of the world. I believe in liberty and freedom is my philosophy. I am not a revolutionary but a pacifist and my weapon is laughter." And when the great man died in 1977, critics everywhere paid homage to an artist who had not only achieved fame in the world of cinema and theater but who had also come to represent a symbol of independence in a world ever more deprived of basic human dignity.

That same image of Chaplin is carefully preserved in Drummond de Andrade's "Canto ao Homem do Povo Charlie Chaplin" ("Song for That Man of the People, Charlie Chaplin"), the last of the forty-eight poems which comprise *A Rosa do Povo*. The Brazilian poet extols Hollywood's most famous clown as a lesson in art and in life, and the initial inspiration for this remarkable poem of tribute is clearly based on a deep sense of affinity and understanding between two men who, although remote in their traditions and circumstances, are nevertheless firmly enjoined in the values they cherish. The "canto" is written in free verse and is skillfully structured into six sections which the poet varies in mood and technique as colloquial intimacy gives way to vigorous rhetoric and moments of tender compassion and fellow-feeling are succeeded by grave philosophical insights.

Drummond de Andrade's canto carries an individual note from the outset. The tone is self-effacing and apologetic as he addresses the world-famous Chaplin, pleading attention and sympathy in a manner which Charlie the tramp will immediately understand. For Drummond de Andrade even in his more limited sphere is also a spokesman for the anonymous, the humble and oppressed. Moreover, he speaks for a remote and neglected Brazil.

While using different artistic means, the filmstar and the poet both seek the same lost virtues—the sanctity and purity of ordinary, everyday things, happenings as simple and sublime as friendship, loyalty and mutual support.

Anxiety and urgency underscore every line of the canto as Drummond de Andrade penetrates the magic of Chaplin's art: "duas horas de anestesia" ("two hours of anaesthesia") and welcome escape from the frustrations and tedium of existence while our screen hero plays *The Champion, The Vagabond, The Immigrant, The Circus Clown,* or *The Pilgrim*—a simple little man of the people in danger of being crushed in a world of giants and supermen yet refusing to throw in the sponge, and on occasion even turning out to be the victor. Mime, emotional involvement, and imagination are the fundamental qualities of Chaplin's art, with its hypnotic ambiguities and suggestive transformations—the symbols of resilience and happiness mingled with the images of nausea, pathos, and suffering. The Brazilian poet salutes in Chaplin our guide to an extraterrestrial world of adventure and enchantment beyond all bureaucracy and tyranny. This fragile creature, who is unmistakable with his bowler hat, walking stick, mustache, and outsize shoes, metamorphoses into a figure of hope and salvation in times of cruel inequalities, and as the canto develops the social and political preoccupations become more intense. The harsh vicissitudes of everyday life are contrasted with the miracles of art; hunger and hallucination overlap; and the coldness and aggression of modern society seem poles apart from the gentleness and vulnerability of Chaplin's lyrical soul.

There is a tragic irony in Chaplin's most significant role as the one pure creature in a corrupt world and the one focal point of unity in a pulverized existence. For Chaplin, as for Drummond de Andrade, only the rediscovery of our true nature as human beings will bring about our salvation in some secret Paradise—"aquele lugar" ("that place") . . . "uma cidade que não sabemos": ("a city we do not know"). Gauche and ridiculous by the world's shabby standards, there is a divine principle inherent in Chaplin, the incurable romantic whose search has much in common with that of the poet when Charlie looks for wild flowers in the gutter or a star's reflection on a dustbin lid.

The canto represents a veritable *tour de force* of poetic art in its own right, and as the closing poem of A Rosa do Povo it also constitutes a synthesis of the themes and moods which color the entire collection.

The poetic techniques exploited in the canto fully conform to the theories set out in the much-quoted "Consideração do Poema" ("Consideration of the Poem") and "Procura de Poesia" ("In Search of Poetry"), wherein the poet defends a poetry without frontiers and therefore free to recover the external world with its multiplicity of things fair and foul. But lest we mistake his intentions, Drummond de Andrade also emphasizes that far from advocating a poetry confined to the description of objects and events or to confession and self-dramatization, he is intent upon a poetry of essence and mystery capable of revealing hidden forms.

The canto also summarizes the entire book as the clearest possible statement of Drummond de Andrade's social commitment on behalf of a confused and spiritually impoverished humanity. A Rosa do Povo abounds in visions of a sorrowful and nauseating world threatened by gathering shadows and languishing in an oppressive climate of collective fear and guilt. Division, destruction, and death have become the natural inheritance of a grasping capitalist society, and the poet can only weep for this "mundo caduco" ("tottering universe"). Life weighs heavily upon him as he struggles to face up to the responsibilities art places upon him: "Sou apenas um homem / Um homem pequenino à beira de um rico / Vejo as aguas que passam e não as compreendo" ("I am only a man / a little man standing on the river bank / I watch the waters pass and cannot understand them") but with Drummond de Andrade every negation ultimately becomes something positive and every apparent failure turns into an achievement. Human isolation, for example, he comes to view as an invaluable lesson in life and solitude itself "uma palavra de amor / não mais um crime, um vício, o desencanto das coisas" ("a word of love / no longer a crime, a vice, the disenchantment of things). Like Chaplin, the poet too must create resources and strategies for salvation even as things perish around him. As artists they must reconstruct and recompose a world mutilated by human greed and folly, thus depriving humanity of poetry and love. So much has already been swept away, yet humble objects and creatures continue to survive from which to initiate the slow and painful task of recovery: "As vezes um botão. Às vezes um rato." ("Sometimes a button. Sometimes a mouse.")

In Chaplin's long film career, we can trace the same growing awareness of the artist's need to feel socially involved. The political parody is self-explanatory in films like *Shoulder Arms* (1918), *City Lights* (1913), *Modern Times* (1936), *The Great Dictator* (1940) and *Monsieur Verdoux* (1947), where warfare, big business, an inhuman machine age, and a society where murderers and thieves flourish are relentlessly attacked.

Yet in both of these prophets of justice and peace, poetry and art prevail over any elements of propaganda. Lyricism and sentiment are rarely suppressed in their pursuit of lost innocence. Both men persist in believing in a world capable of agreeable surprises and in secret territories waiting to be explored: both are ready to hasten "para onde os telegramas estão chamando" ("wherever telegrams may summon them"). Both seek to capture and reveal all that is worthwhile in life and to render its essence intelligible whatever the cost, for as Drummond de Andrade reminds us: "Tal uma inteligência do universo / comprada em sal, em rugos e cabelo" ("Such knowledge of the universe / is purchased in salt, wrinkles and hair"). And both are intrepid in their search for a new dimension "onde è tudo belo e fantástico" ("where everything is beautiful and fantastic")—and speak of redemption.

I
It had to be a poet from Brazil
not one of the greatest, but one most vulnerable to ridicule,
revolving somewhat in your atmosphere or aspiring to live therein
as in the poetic and essential orbit of lucid dreams,

it had to be this obstinate little poet
of elementary rhythms, fresh from a small provincial town
where ties are rarely worn but people are extremely civil,
where oppression is loathed, though heroism is tinged with irony,

it had to be this former youth of twenty,
drawn to your pantomime by threads of affection and laughter
    dispersed in time,
who should come to reunite them, and as a mature man, pay you
    a visit
to confide certain things, under the guise of a poem.

To tell you how we Brazilians love you
and how in this, as in everything else, our people are like
any other people in the world—even the little Jews
with walking stick and bowler hat, pointed shoes and mournful eyes,

tramps whom the world has spurned, but they go on living
    and jesting
in films, on crooked streets with signboards: Factory, Barber,
    Police,
fighting off hunger, avoiding violence and prolonging love
like a secret whispered into the ear of some fellow creature lying
    in the gutter.

I know that speeches with smooth bourgeois sentiments
    leave you unmoved,
and that you are wont to sleep while impassioned souls
    inaugurate statues,
and that among so many words traveling the roads like motorcars,
only the humblest, expressing rebuke or endearment, can touch you.

I do not offer the tribute or a fan or partisan
for these are shortlived, but the simple greeting of an ordinary
    man living in an ordinary town,

nor can I extol the substance of this song I weave around you
like a bouquet of absurd flowers despatched by mail to the inventor
    of gardens.

I speak for those sullied by grief and a violent distaste
        for everything,
who have invaded the cinema like an affliction of rats escaping life,
two hours of anaesthesia—let's listen to some music,
see images in the dark—instead they discovered you and were saved.

I speak for those deserted by justice, for the simple of heart,
outcasts, bankrupts, the fractured and inadequate, losers,
the oppressed, the lonely and indecisive, poets and dreamers,
the childish and irresponsible, for those starved of love,
        for fools and madmen.

I speak for the flowers you cherish once trampled,
for those candlestumps you eat in extreme poverty, for the table,
        buttons,
the instruments of your trade and the thousand and one things
        seemingly impenetrable,
each gadget, each object salvaged from the attic, ever obscure
        yet eloquent.

II
Your clothes are the color of night.
A darkness unrelieved by your spotted waistcoat
or your gelid dress shirt donned festively
for an impossible dance without orchids.
You are condemned to wearing black. Your trousers
merge with the shadows. Your shoes,
swollen in the darkness of the alley
become nocturnal toadstools. Your quasi-tophat,
a black sun, enshrouds everything, without rays.
Thus nocturnal citizen of a republic
in mourning, you arise before our pessimistic
eyes, which inspect you and meditate:
Behold the downcast creature, the widower beyond consolation,
the raven, the nevermore, the late arrival
in a world grown old.

And the moon alights
on your face. Stark white, chalked with death,
evoking sepulchers, petrified submarine algae and mirrors
and lilies desecrated by some tyrant, and visages
covered in flour. The black
mustache grows on you like an omen
suddenly interrupted. It is black, short
and thick. Oh white mask of lunar substance,
mask cut from linen, tracing on a wall,
a childish sketch, barely an image,
yet the eyes are sunken and the mouth comes from afar,
isolated, knowing and silent, the mouth forms
a smile, and dawn breaks for everyone.

Now we no longer feel the night.
Death avoids us, and we grow small,
as if at the stroke of your magic cane, we were restored
to the secret land where children slumber.
It is no longer the office with a thousand files,
the garage, the university, the alarm clock,
it is truly the abolished street, shops crammed with wares,
and off we go to break windows,
to knock the watchman to the ground
to rediscover in the human species
that spot—look out!—which attracts a swift kick in the pants:
      the sentence
of an arbitrary justice.

III
Full of nourishing suggestions, you quell the hunger
of those who have not been summoned to the celestial or
industrial supper. There are bones, blancmanges,
cherries, chocolates and clouds
in the folds of your jacket. Rescued
for some child or stray dog. For you appreciate
the importance of food, the taste of meat,
the aroma of soup, the yellow softness of potato,
and you have mastered the subtle art of transforming your humble

shoelaces into spaghetti.
Once again you have managed to eat: life is just fine.
Time for a cigarette: and you take one
from your sardine tin.

There are all too few dinners in the world as you well know,
and the most inviting chickens
are covered by glass domes over china platters.
There is always glass, and it never breaks,
there is steel, asbestos, the law,
an entire militia protecting that chicken,
and a hunger blowing all the way from Canada, a wind,
a glacial voice, the breath of winter, a leaf
hovering indecisively, alights on your shoulder: an indistinct
    message
that you can barely decipher. Between the chicken and hunger
there is unbreakable glass. Between the hand and hunger
the barriers of the law and infinite space. Then you transform
into a great roast chicken suspended in mid air
above all hungers; chicken of burnished gold
and flame, a feast for all
on a day for all, but it is slow in coming.

IV
The New Year itself is late. And so are the lovers.
At the solitary fête your talents crystallize.
You are incorporeal and fluent, a ballet dancer,
but no one will venture here to see how you love
with the ardor of diamonds and the delicacy of dawn,
how the shack, at your touch, becomes the moon.
A world of snow and salt, of raucous gramophones
screaching in the distance some pleasure you cannot share.
A forbidden world, imprisoning lovers
and all desire for communication in its night.
Your palace evaporates, sleep overcomes you,
rejected by all. Everyone possesses something
and you tried to give all, only to be spurned.

Haunted by cold indifference, you observe the revels from afar
but feel no appetite for the feast, nor pride
nor pain nor rage nor malice.
You are the New Year itself, lingering on. The house goes by
running, glasses go flying,
bodies suddenly take flight, lovers
seek you in the night but fail to recognize you
. . . so tiny,
so simple, so ordinary.

To be so lonely amidst so many shoulders,
to walk by the thousands in a single, puny frame,
and stretch enormous arms over the houses,
to have one foot in Guerrero and the other in Texas,
to speak as easily to a Chinaman as to an Amazonian,
a Russian or an African: to be alone, yet belonging to all,
without word or philter,
or opal:
there is a city within you, we do not know.

V
A blind woman loves you. Her eyes open.
No, she loves you not. A rich man, inebriated,
becomes your friend, but once sober, he scorns
your riches. The confusion is ours, for we forget
what there is of water, breeze and innocence
at the heart of every earthly mortal. But, oh, the myths
that we falsely worship: drab flowers,
disloyal angels, circular coffers, solemn
and poetic croakings: conventions
in red, white and blue; machinery,
series of telegrams, factory upon factory
upon factory of lamps, prohibitions and auroras.
You were only a common workman
controlled by an irate voice booming into a megaphone.
You are a mere cog, a gesture, a grimace.
I gather up the pieces: they still vibrate,
a mutilated lizard.

I paste your pieces together. Yours
is a strange unity in a pulverized world.
And we, who with every step, cover ourselves,
undress and mask ourselves,
rarely encounter you in the same guise,
                    apprentice
                    fireman
                    accountant
                    confectioner
                    immigrant
                    convict
                    machinist
                    bridegroom
                    skater
                    soldier
                    musician
                    pilgrim
                    circus performer
                    marquis
                    sailor
                    piano remover
Yet meanwhile, ever yourself,
the man who refuses to conform although ever so gentle,
incapable of ownership, restless
for the open road
and freedom, the friend
whom we should like to detain
in the drizzle, the mirror, our memory,
only to lose him.

VI
I no longer think about you. I think about the trade
you practice. Mysterious watchmaker,
you smell of dismantled pieces: the springs unite
and time starts up. You clean windows.
You sweep roads. Who cares if the longing
to be off devours you; if the next corner
changes you into another man; if logic

excludes you from its calculated privileges.
There is work in you, but capricious
and benign,
creating arts that are alien to the bourgeoisie,
the products of air and tears, apparel
that presents us with petals or wings, trains
and ships built without steel, where friends
by forming a circle, travel through time,
books come to life, paintings converse,
and everything released dissolves
in an effusion of unrequited love, smiles and sunshine.

Your trade is the trade
which puts you in our midst,
a vagabond between two timetables; a hand skilled
at hammering, sawing, weaving and plastering,
your foot insists upon taking you around the world,
your hand picks up an instrument: this time a razor,
and to the music of Brahms you shave away
in this forgetful saloon at the center of an oppressed world
where after so much emptiness and silence, we recover you.

It was as well that you should be silent.
You meditated in the shadow of locks,
chains, striped clothing, barbed-wire fences,
you attracted harsh words, stones, cement, bombs, invectives,
with a secret pencil you recorded the death of thousands,
      the blood-stained mouth
of thousands, the crossed arms of thousands.
And you said nothing. A lump, a nausea
gathering. Words forming.
Oh demoralized words, yet redeemed and uttered anew.
The power of the human voice inventing new words and
      reviving others.
The dignity of your mouth, open in just anger and deep love,
a twitching of the body, a writhing tree, rebelling against
      the baseness and fury of dictators,
Oh Charlie, mine and everybody's friend, your shoes and mustache
      walk a road of dust and expectation.

IN THE MIND'S EYE

JOE ASHBY PORTER

When she graduated from high school Doris Fulkerson, valedictorian of her class and the only child of a prosperous widower, married Arnold Barron who was somewhat below her. The Barron blood was reckless. Arnold's father had eked out a living with a little gas station, but Arnold himself was ambitious. During World War I he took Doris off to Canada. He had a complicated scheme for making easy money from the war, but luck was against him, and after Doris became pregnant he caught pneumonia and died. Doris had barely enough cash and self-possession for the long journey home to Kentucky. When she arrived she discovered that her father too had died and that the war had ruined his business. As far as she knew she had no relatives anywhere, and certainly none in the town, which had turned against her on account of Arnold's wild venture. All that was left her was a small farm just outside the city limits. She sold half the land and then, living in the farmhouse, went into a seclusion to wait out her pregnancy and to think about what could be done with the rest of her life. She decided to take in laundry and to make use of her education by dealing in junk which she would call antiques.

When labor started she summoned a midwife and drank bourbon until she was unconscious. She awoke to discover she had given birth to twin boys. For ten dollars extra the midwife (who supposed that scandal was involved and the infants would be disposed of in

63

some illegal fashion) agreed to maintain silence. Within the week Doris went to the courthouse to register the birth of a son, Victor, named after her father. This was in early June 1918.

Carefully and in some desperation she had estimated the expenses of raising one child, and she held to her plans regardless of facts as they were. She could have dispatched one of them with impunity, but her solution was less direct, more imaginative, and perhaps kinder. She simply recognized the existence of each on alternate days. Every other day each lived a normal life downstairs with her while upstairs his brother lay in the small rear bedroom ignored. She would interchange them in the early morning when they were still asleep and when she herself was as it were insufficiently conscious of what was happening.

Thus from the beginning, far prior to the reach of their memories, the twins were molded by an extraordinary pattern of life. One day each existed properly as a creature in his mother's attention only to return the following day to a suspended animation. They survived infancy because they were very hardy. Each of course was called Victor.

During what we may term the days of recognition each passed an agreeable time with Doris. Without regard to their age she discussed with them the most complex and adult matters as she cared for them or went about her housework, so that they commanded a large and sophisticated vocabulary. In her talks with them Doris returned most often to two subjects, their father and the community. From some necessity of her mind Arnold had become for her an ideal figure quite unlike the man she had married. She presented him to the twins as a fabulous inventor inspired with sacred genius; she made an apotheosis of his premature death. When she spoke of the community she emphasized its cruelty and its power.

School was the twins' first important contact with the world outside Doris's influence. They were suspicious and aggressive. Because neither had much use for other children it was some years before they began to perceive the peculiarities of their situation. They attended school, as they had done everything else, on alternate days. Since they were physically identical no one suspected that there were two Victors. Both were precocious, but fairly early their interests began to develop in different directions, the one toward science, particularly mathematics, the other toward the humanities, particularly literature. It meant that "Victor," according to his teachers, was brilliant but erratic.

Doris had realized that, given the situation, words such as "yesterday" and "tomorrow" were bound to cause trouble, and therefore she avoided them. Thus in their childhood the twins were to an abnormal degree spared the idea of time. Such as they had, they would have developed primitively on their own with almost no help from the embodiment of the idea in the language. Matters were different at school. Inextricably mixed with all the other shocks of their first contact with the community were the teacher's magical outlandish words, "And tomorrow, children. . . ." It was easy enough to learn the names of the weekdays, but the reason for the order in which they were taught was unclear to the twins, for whom the order naturally ran Sunday Tuesday Thursday Saturday etc. They asked no one for help with these problems, especially not Doris, whom they loved and revered. But they began to feel that the world had huge mysteries in store for them.

Children are all conservative, and the twins were unusually so: through the first six years of their lives it occurred to neither to break with time-honored routine by seizing an opportunity—when Doris was out of the house—to climb the stairs and explore the little bedroom. But the confusion spawned by school made them adventurous, and at last it happened. One winter afternoon Victor opened the door to find himself peeping sleepily out from a pile of blankets; Victor awoke from a nap to see himself standing in the open doorway. They stared at one another for several minutes. Then one closed his eyes and retreated beneath the blankets, and one closed the door and ran downstairs.

It was so miraculous that for days they dared not hope for a repetition. One lay upstairs never turning his face toward the doorway; downstairs the other avoided the vicinity of the stair. But the strain was too great to last. This time instead of hiding or retreating they faced one another alike smiling a little doubtfully. They touched one another for reassurance. There was a corner of the backyard which, because it was in view of the back bedroom window, Doris had fenced off and forbidden them to enter. She had strung up a clothesline there, and it was where she then stood, struggling to gather in a wash that had frozen. The twins watched her until she returned to the house, and then one of them slipped downstairs. They had not said anything, but they had reached some understanding.

In the dead of the next morning when Doris rose to exchange the twins she found Victor's bed, beside her own, empty. Almost immediately Victor entered the room to say, "Don't worry. It's all right." Thenceforth the twins themselves carried out the ritual exchange. Doris must have been obscurely aware that they had discovered one another, had found her out. But there was an enormous compensation: she no longer needed by any of her actions to recognize that there were two. Her madness had been accommodated. Her sons had taken it upon themselves and left her free for perfect consistency. From this time she seemed to take heart—the community remarked on it. There was a gala opening of her shop with a banner redundantly proclaiming "Mrs. Barron's Unique Antiques: No Two of Anything." It was something of a success. Not yet willing to befriend her, the local women nevertheless patronized her readily.

Now the twins spent much of their time together in the bedroom upstairs. They had a great deal to think over so that for some weeks they did not talk. It was a milestone when one said, "Miss Tackett asked me to recite the alphabet at school," and the other asked, "Did I do it right?" Once initiated, this form of communication (it was after all in a sense the logical one) prevailed. They never addressed one another in the second person, but always used the first, and always the singular. The peculiarity of their language manifested a genuine and deep peculiarity of thought. They simply did not conceive of themselves as distinct from one another in the way they were distinct from everyone else.

They knew Doris was not in their situation since there was no room in the house for any alter ego of hers. It did occur to them that other children might be like them. The evidence was against it —the fact that they alone had confused the order of the week— but for a long time they harbored the suspicion. Visiting their friends they would find excuses for exploring a home from top to bottom.

(Circumstances provided them with an innocuous introduction to the word "twin." There happened to be in the town a pair of nonidentical twins, a boy and a girl a few years older than "Victor." To Victor, then, twins were simply siblings who chanced to be the same age. It had nothing to do with their own case—indeed they did not think of themselves as separate enough to be siblings.)

"I didn't make any mistakes on the spelling test did I? What was the arithmetic assignment? Did I have fun at recess?" Doris had determined that the rear bedroom would be Victor's playroom and study; the twins spent their afternoons and evenings there talking, preparing their lesson from the same book. On rare occasions when a visiting schoolmate asked what was behind the door at the end of the hallway he was told that the room was an empty closet; the door was locked from the inside. As far as Doris was concerned the room may as well not have existed, for she no longer even came near the door. So with always greater caution the twins guarded the received status. "We played red rover—my team won. There's no arithmetic. I had a perfect spelling score—no one else did—Shirley missed 'cemetery.' "

Their secret would probably have been discovered if they had been engaged in a direct deception of the community, but they had no such simple intent. They did have a kind of secret but it was not the sort anyone was likely to suspect. It was not even something that could very easily be revealed. Already in their childhood the task of finding a way of publicizing the matter—finding words in the common tongue for it—would have been greater than the task of maintaining a vigilance to gloss over minor awkwardnesses. If something like duplicity was occasionally necessary, it was far more often the case that they told in good faith the only truth they could. "How does it happen that you do so much better than the other students, Victor?" asked one of their teachers. "I think," said Victor, "it's partly because my father was a genius, and then partly because I never think about just one thing at a time." The teacher repeated Victor's answer to friends as evidence of his originality.

The very idea of thought was difficult enough. The twins always believed that their minds were not completely separate, but it had become clear that they were in a sense divided. Both a cause and a consequence of this discovery was the fact that they grew less idle during the time they spent in the little bedroom. They thought about things; they read such books as they could find to interest them in the drafty run-down county public library. And, having learned to talk to one another, they progressed naturally to the ability to talk to themselves. (There were thus for each some four grades of conversation: with the community, with Doris, with his alter ego, and with himself, in order of increasing privacy. Grammatically, of course, the first two differed little and the last two were almost indistinguishable. Lexically their conversation with Doris differed from the other three: it was now only here that a vocabulary for dealing with time was absent. It may be this that made her endure in their minds, intense and fresh, even when they were adults.)

Their interests and abilities began to diverge as soon as they discovered that they had "sort of . . . two minds," at about age eleven in 1929 as the stock market crashed. One was drawn more to the exact sciences and the other to the humanities. The division was never absolute, and as adults each remained au courant with the other's field. But once begun, the specialization was bound to increase if only because it was very profitable. "Victor," who had been an outstanding student, grew prodigious. For the next several years the slightly hushed tones in which her customers spoke of Victor made Doris herself whisper in her mind when she thought about her son. She stopped fondling him, she listened carefully to whatever he said.

When it came to fostering his talents she was at a loss. It remained to one of his teachers in secondary school (an ancient lady who taught him Caesar and Virgil and geometry) to take positive action. Largely as a result of her guidance Victor went off in the fall of '36 on the train to Boston and Cambridge, to the august Harvard College. Doris was prostrated with grief at his departure. The stationmaster said Victor himself seemed nervous: "He'd be sitting in the waiting room and the next thing I knew he'd be outside fidgeting around on the platform. And then when the train stopped he kept getting on and then getting back off, two or three times." The twins were in fact excited but they were not in the least frightened. As in separate cars they watched the changing terrain their thoughts were of their mother and of the triumphs of which they were by then fairly confident.

At first Harvard disappointed them. Perhaps they harbored some expectation of finding there at least others in their situation. In any case their disappointment was with the student body, which seemed to differ not in kind but merely in degree from the schoolmates they had left behind. Still, the competition was sufficient to force a much greater specialization on them. The schedule of their alternation had to grow flexible—they might make the change several times a day.

Harvard itself during these years was in a transition. Victor Barron was one of the new breed that within a decade or two would dominate the college—the provincials, scholarship students of unknown families, drawn to New England out of nameless towns lost across the country, eager young men with nothing to recommend them but sheer learning and ability. Because almost everyone supposed Victor represented the thing coming for better or worse, they watched him with special interest. Despite the bustle of expansion and new building, Harvard in its flow of gossip and speculation was still much like the village the twins had left behind. It was soon clear to the community that Victor Barron was an article rather different from his fellow provincials. His success seemed effortless, nor was he apparently very ambitious. His form was eccentric rather than bad. Therefore he penetrated circles normally closed to his sort and so became familiar with the ways of the privileged. And when Victor was diffident in the face of social as well as academic success people concluded that he was not merely odd but also subtle and deep.

Meanwhile Doris became more ordinary. Expecting her to put on airs, people had hung back for a while after Victor's acceptance to Harvard was announced in the local newspaper. In fact, however, the clipping had come as the complete justification of her life, obviating further haughtiness. Victor had been launched, and grieved, she had done her part; now she settled down to make peace and enjoy the rest of her life. Her replies to the profuse daily letters from her son grew perfunctory. When he wrote that he was doing research into the logic of relations, the philosophy of individualism, the figure of the Doppelganger, she returned her gracious approval though she had not an inkling of the meaning of his phrases. When acquaintances asked after him the information they received was agreeably vague—"No, no he doesn't have any particular young lady I don't imagine. I think he really has the bachelor's temperament— you know how these absent-minded scholars are." She was quiet, chatty, and considerate. She renewed friendships of her schooldays. She thought of remarrying or taking a vacation.

The progress of the twins' specialization was as follows: One narrowed his interest in science to a concentration in mathematics, thence to the "foundations of mathematics," logic and set theory, and finally he settled in the difficult and then modish discipline of philosophy of mathematics. The direction of the other was a sort of mirror image—from the humanities in general to the study of literature, to aesthetic philosophy. Both in their final years at college proved able creators as well as scholars. In the fall of 1940 ominous with World War II there appeared in various Cambridge magazines and journals four works by V. Barron: an evaluation of Wittgenstein, a re-evaluation of Aristotle's *Poetics*, a work of original mathematics entitled "Prediction in Unfolding Sequences of the Form 01101001 . . . ," and "Mr. Hyde," a group of four witty and scandalous sonnets.

Doris's ease and her increasingly pleasant relations with the community produced a late bloom in her. Lines of strain vanished, she grew plump and even pretty. Therefore, and because the town had begun to realize that after the years of frugality she must have had a substantial sum tucked away, a number of prosperous middle-aged bachelors and widowers began to court her. It meant that with hints dropped here and there she was able to perform a considerable service for the twins entirely without their knowledge. They were puzzled by the announcement that Victor Barron had been deferred from the draft for reasons of health, but they did not resent it. Unlike most of their contemporaries they were not eager to defend their country; furthermore romance at last loomed on the horizon.

The first year at Harvard had been monastic, but the second saw the awakening of their interest in their Radcliffe classmates. They learned a great deal from a flirtation with Melissa and Felicia Machemer, identical twins from the Maine woods. In the back of Victor's mind was the timid hope that these shy pretty girls might have coped with a situation like his own. Communication in any case proved a greater problem than he expected. By this time, to be sure, the twins had seen the possibility of talking about, and to one another with, the system of pronouns they used for the rest of humankind. "It would ease my relations with the community in some ways," one said to the other, "but although they would think me suddenly more honest I should feel suddenly less so. The violence would be too great if I began speaking of myself as 'him and me' or to myself as 'you and I.' The words simply aren't honest or proper after all—they don't fit. Still, there will be difficulties with

Felicia and Melissa." Difficulties there were, and the episode added to Victor's reputation for eccentricity, for Felicia and Melissa were voluble in their amazement. "At first we thought he was playing some joke. He practically hinted he had considered proposing to . . . *us both!*"

(One of the difficulties of telling their story is that much of what most aptly characterizes them seems trivial or even disagreeable—throughout their lives they felt most comfortable in the vicinity of mirrors. When as adults they thought back on their history the whole thing seemed to have an odor they remembered from youth: the chalk dust that lingered in empty classrooms through winter afternoons. It had the air of a childish and vacuous didacticism poignant even when it set the teeth on edge. They sometimes seemed not like men but like thin girls.)

Upon arriving in Cambridge they had found rooms in a pleasant out-of-the-way narrow street; and since it had no longer been necessary for them to have two beds, they had one. In the beginning they slept together in the same spirit in which they had slept apart, but matters changed after Melissa's and Felicia's shocked failure to comprehend. They were well aware of the various categories of vice but had always maintained an effortless innocence, a sort of meditative distance. Now however one's hands wandered to the other as they lay side by side half awake. Still, they could not tell whether what they had discovered was vice or not: what they did together they would not have dreamed of doing alone or with another man. But they did not trouble themselves much with definition, and their passion followed its course unrestrained, accelerating until it absorbed them entirely and then subsiding to perfunctoriness and finally dwindling to almost nothing, all in the course of a month.

Such then was the background for their great love. Marie-Christine Dolanyi was one of those waifs of ambiguously aristocratic family who find their way to the Boston academy from all parts of the world. She had been born in Paris of generally Hungarian parents and had spent most of her life in London and New York. Her motley and exotic history augured well, the twins thought. Because she was thin and sallow and wore her hair long and pulled back, she had a certain questionable chic, but her features were not extraordinary; all this too seemed promising. Still the twins avoided rushing into explanations of their situation, and they put off hints of anything so serious as marriage.

It went well. Marie-Christine was friendly and talkative; she and Victor enjoyed one another's company. She was a student of art history and aimed to be an architect, so that her interests nicely complemented those of both the twins. More important, her psychological and moral stance was as special as theirs though, as became evident, from different causes: where they sought that elusive set of consistent rules and standards adequate to their situation, Marie-Christine was discovering that she could cheerfully forgo any such quest and enjoy not being able to predict what she might do from one moment to the next. The twins thought this the best omen of all.

In their letters to their mother they hesitated to mention Marie-Christine. Looking back on Doris through a considerable distance in time and space and experience, they had begun to reflect on her attitude toward them and to find it mysterious. A question they had never given much thought to now demanded attention: in what way exactly did their mother understand their position? It seemed eerily possible that she might view them in a way not very different from the rest of the world. They believed they could recall a time when she had supervised their daily interchange, and yet this might be an illusion. And yet—and yet there must have been a time, they reasoned, when she had supervised everything. But just this period was entirely beyond the reach of their memories. Their speculations gave them the odd feeling of having almost created themselves while at the same time paradoxically calling to their minds the bright shadowy figure of their father.

They sent Doris an experimental letter mentioning their interest in Marie-Christine. Doris's reply made no reference to the information. When at length they wrote more Doris replied, "I am interested to hear all your news." They wondered whether the increasing vagueness of her letters had been a strategic preparation for the moment at hand. They wondered, but they elected not to rush things with Doris any more than with Marie-Christine, and in their own letters they began to observe a careful silence regarding their romance.

In fact Doris's silence was partly studied. Her son's first mention of the girl had made her more uneasy than anything he had said before. At first she accused herself of a mother's selfishness. "After all," she told herself, "he does have to live his own life," and this consideration relieved her for a day or two. Yet when it came time to write Victor she found herself unable to speak of the matter. Perhaps it was her musing over the possibility of marrying again herself, or the fact that she had at last found a very secure and pleasant place for herself in the little community so that she could afford some unprecedented freedom in her own thoughts—for whatever reason, she began to wonder whether all was well with her son. "Maybe I've been unrealistic," she said to herself, "maybe I've idolized him too much." And she said to her close friend Hattie Partridge, "It's strange, he's my own son but I feel as if I don't know him. I can't help but think he'd wrong a wife somehow. Without meaning it, of course." Hattie couldn't conceal the fact that the statement seemed bizarre to her. Thereafter Doris kept her forebodings to herself, but they continued to trouble her. For a long time she had viewed her son much as the rest of the world did; but now as it were with a change in the weather the old self-inflicted injury to her sanity was acting up.

Marie-Christine moved into the apartment on Shepard Street in the fall of the twins' second year. It was to their advantage that she was absent-minded as well as chaotic and free and also that she had an incongruous sense of propriety: for the sake of appearance she kept an apartment of her own and gave a key to her lover. An old pattern asserted itself. Each of the twins slept one night in his own bed with Marie-Christine and the next alone in hers. She was everything they could have wanted, she was lazy and perfect. As early as ten they would trudge home from the library through the deep wet snow to find her asleep on the sofa before the fire.

A consequence of their liaison was that they saw less of one another than ever before. This mere physical separation affected them quite as strongly as their departure from Kentucky had done; but the effects were more subtle and gradual. Sometimes the separations lasted more than a week. In the climate of unorthodox speculation inaugurated by Doris's silence on the subject of Marie-Christine the twins began, only half voluntarily, to see their situation in new lights—a sort of aurora borealis seemed to play in both their minds. Especially during those minutes of the morning when they lay not yet fully awake beside Marie-Christine, odd perspectives would open. For instance each might have the sensation that the other was little more than a figment of his imagination, a persistent dream.

And each began to consider the other's discipline from the stand-point of his own. The question they framed was, "What is to be done about . . . ." One completed it with "fiction" and the other with "logic." Whichever question was broached to Marie-Christine, she shrugged and said, "Why not worry about the real world." Their replies were much the same: "The real world takes care of itself." Marie-Christine said, "It's letting Hitler take care of it!"

The twins were in complete accord with her dismay; indeed they in their innocence were far more profoundly shocked than she who for most of her life had been intimately affected by vagaries of inter-national politics. But for them the fact that the world was letting Hitler take care of it proved the irrelevance of personal action. There was nothing they could do. The problem, while presenting itself in terms of the practical, seemed immune to any attack in such terms—it seemed to lift itself by its own bootstraps into the realm of the theoretical. To them it was thereby more, not less, serious. And it was almost inevitable that they should see this problem in relation to the other that absorbed them. Thus there were times when each saw the other's chosen discipline as a force aiming at universal dictatorship, its demands granted through a policy of appeasement; and there were times when each saw his own discipline so.

Their concern for what might be called the international politics of the mind partly bridged the new distance between them occa-sioned by the mechanics of living with Marie-Christine. As though for a series of diplomatic talks they began to seek one another out; their talks were successful because they spoke in good faith unlike real diplomats. It turned out that something more exciting than peaceful coexistence was possible and even, as they thought, neces-sary. What was indicated was for the disciplines to renew them-selves by subsuming one another, since their aims finally converged. Literature and philosophy were to become more like one another, especially in their format: investigating philosophical problems was to involve constructing fictions and vice versa. In all this the twins were children of their time more than they knew.

Their rapprochement began in the winter and lasted into spring with every promise of continuing indefinitely. Marie-Christine sus-pected Victor of philandering: the occasional untruthfulness with which they glossed over the time they spent together failed with her. And yet she was not jealous—in fact she was pleased to think of her young man's gaining a bit of what seemed to her salutary experience. And she had nothing to complain of since his attentions to her were if anything increased. She was beginning to realize that Victor was very satisfactory indeed, and she was considering the possibilities of a long-term association with him. Thus all three of them felt pleasantly on the verge of something as the Cambridge weather made its fitful and lovely progress toward summer.

In May, excited and fortified by these developments, the twins renewed their attempt to elicit from Doris some formal recognition of Marie-Christine. Since strong measures seemed needed they went a little beyond the facts and spoke of a probable engagement. After a week's silence came a reply. The twins read it together.

"I expect you have wondered that I've not said anything about your young lady before this. Well, it was partly that I didn't quite know what to say. Then too I felt it would be wiser to wait a bit in case she was merely the sort of passing fancy young men seem so prone to nowadays. (I've tried to think what your father would have done.) I see now that your interest in her is not at all frivolous.

"I should also say, Victor, that I have been a touch uneasy to think of your marrying—but we'll talk about that when I see you— you're just so unique I have a hard time trying to imagine what sort of wife would be right for you—I hope you'll write and tell me more about Marie-Christine—but we'll talk. In fact we've a great deal to talk about.

"I had hoped to come to Cambridge for your graduation and to meet Marie but I'm afraid it won't be possible. I haven't been as well as I should be—don't alarm yourself, I haven't mentioned it because it's nothing very serious—but Dr. Finley says I ought not make the trip. Maybe it's for the best, as I'm not sure I'd know how to behave among all those people up there. Still, it's a great disappointment. I'll be glad to send a letter of explanation if there's any sort of ceremony that requires my attendance.

"But I have thought of a plan to make up for this. I suppose you intend to come home to visit for some part of the summer. And so I would like you to invite Marie to come with you, so that we can get to know one another. She could stay in the back bedroom, or I could arrange other lodgings for her—whatever is convenient. I don't know just how much rail tickets cost now, but I've enclosed a check that ought to cover your fares at least. I want this trip to be my graduation present to you.

"I know this place won't seem very exciting to a young lady familiar with the capitals of Europe—but if you can convince her to come, I'll do what I can to divert her."

One of the twins said, "It's reassuring . . ." and the other continued ". . . but somehow not so much as I'd expected." Doris's check was generous—the total something above the price of three round-trip tickets.

Marie-Christine had planned to spend the summer with friends on Long Island, but she was easily persuaded to come to Kentucky, which seemed as exotic to her as Europe seemed to Victor. Further, an instinct told her that meeting Mrs. Barron would reveal much about Victor. The twins by this time were such virtuosos at juggling themselves on trains that Marie-Christine's presence simply added zest to the performance. Yet as the train pulled out of South Station they looked out on Boston with a nervous melancholy. More than ever before in making this trip they seemed to be leaving a world of brisk airy freedom and returning to a region fenced with the dumb rigors of the heart. There might not after all be room for Marie-Christine, they thought.

The house had been refurbished top to bottom—fresh paint, modish new drapes, and everywhere the "antiques"—ink bottles on the mantelpiece, trivets and serving trays and other kitchenware on the walls, a bouquet of Gramophone speakers in a corner, and a genuine cowcatcher on the hearth. Doris seemed timid but ceremonious and efficient. By a stroke of luck her neighbor Frieda Kirkwood was away for the summer, leaving her house vacant. Marie-Christine could stay there. Victor could return to his old room and use the back bedroom for a study—there was still a bed there if he wanted a nap. The old Dodge had been repaired so that the young people could visit scenic spots in the area.

The first days passed in a clutter of arrangements and obligatory social calls. Doris bided her time and attempted no more than the most polite small talk with Marie-Christine; but she watched with interest. Though the community was awed by the girl's accent and her foreign manners, when she turned out to be "not on her high horse one bit" but friendly and rather open, they were charmed.

Doris too was beginning to be charmed. "Whatever she does she looks as if she's in a picture," Doris said to Victor, and there was a wistful fall in her voice.

One of the twins was always at the Kirkwood house reading, writing, or daydreaming. In the evenings he would slip out to wait in the dark for an hour and then re-enter pretending he had crept away from his own house. They alternated regularly. The time spent alone was especially thankful as a relief from contact with the townspeople. The twins were not entirely pleased with Doris's new sociability—her reconciliation with the community seemed to compromise her a little in their eyes. And they would have preferred it if people had taken to Marie-Christine less readily.

As things quieted, Doris and Marie-Christine sought occasions to be alone together. At first the twins encouraged this both because they were curious to see how the women would react to each other given a chance for greater intimacy and because it enabled them (the twins) to be together.

Doris was thirty-eight, and she had decorated herself, manner and body, with gewgaws somewhat like those cluttering her house. Marie-Christine in the full flower of her youth was easygoing to the point of being streamlined. They sat in the kitchen and sipped coffee. By fits and starts Doris tried to sound out Marie-Christine on the subject of Victor. The girl was friendly but, it seemed to Doris, noncommittal. Doris fished with "I think you must be the first young lady he's taken a genuine interest in." Marie-Christine chuckled. Doris raised her eyebrows and watered her African violets.

"He was very much out of the ordinary here, as you might imagine. I suppose some people found him . . . peculiar, or . . ." Doris said. Marie-Christine nodded and said, "I think some people in Cambridge found him peculiar also. May I ask, does this surprise you?" "Not exactly . . ." In a moment Doris said, "Won't you have some more coffee, Marie, and listen to a word of wisdom, such as it is, or advice. You young people appear to have become fairly well . . . infatuated, haven't you? What I would suggest (I hope you take this in the spirit in which it's meant) is that it would be well for you to . . . scrutinize one another a little more carefully. Young people who are admirable in themselves don't always have altogether the best effect on one another; in spite of their good intentions. I suspect there's a great deal you don't know about Victor—a great deal no one knows. . . ." "You sound almost ominous!" "Yes, I do," said Doris.

Marie-Christine's curiosity was aroused. She described the conversation to Victor. "What do you suppose?" she said, "—that it's really me she's worried about, and not you? We *have* 'scrutinized' each other more than she knows, haven't we? You know, I do like her—far more than I'd expected to, and I can't help but be troubled by this mysterious anxiety of hers. Victor, let's stay here for the summer—I feel as though she might need some help we could give her."

I have related the foregoing as if I were some sort of semi-detached observer, partly because it seemed that only through such a fiction could I set forth the events described so that they would be comprehensible to the ordinary reader. However I think by now the fiction (wearisome to me from the beginning) has served its purpose and can safely be abandoned, so that I shall henceforth speak in my own voice and from my own viewpoint. I hope the relief I feel won't lead me into unnecessary expansiveness. But I do want to try to be faithful to things as they happened. I wrote the preceding section in bits and scraps during July. It is now the second week in September, and since I have no immediate plans I should be able to finish the story in a day or two. I am still rather in a daze, and this writing may help dissipate some of the shock and clear my mind.

What stands out most in my memory of these past weeks like an emblem for everything else that happened is Marie-Christine's face, which seemed to grow lovelier as it showed more strain, bewilderment, and fatigue—as though she were a flower whose delicacy was manifest only in its wilting. While the sun browned Mother and me it seemed to bleach her skin—by the first of September she was paler than I had ever seen her—the very blue of her eyes looked lighter.

The whole thing seems to shift and fall apart and regroup in my mind as I think back on it—we all somewhat lost our self-possession, we all grew somewhat feverish and harried, and now I feel weak and drained but relieved. The paper predicts a week's rain—it is raining now, a slow chilly rain. I have lighted a fire—I feel weak, but since I am both ambidextrous I can shift the writing among four hands. I shall clear my mind and begin while the fire burns and the rain falls. I shall finish the tale. Perhaps it is hardly necessary: perhaps the conclusion was foredestined and is apparent to the discerning eye—in general, at least—the peculiar alloy of triumph and failure. But the particulars are of interest, and I shall finish the tale.

Boston now seemed a sweet romance. The future had begun to rush and to demand decisions to fill its vacancy. I felt my age—I felt it was time for me to reap some comfort and security after my long adventure. I did not want to have much to do with the "real world," but I did want a certain minimum ideally embodied, I thought, in Marie-Christine. I would certainly have wished to give Mother any help I could, "but not," as I told myself, "at the expense of my entire happiness." Still I could not very gracefully bustle Marie-Christine off, and so I agreed to stay. If the summer proved an ordeal I would meet it with the assurance that it would be the crucial one. And I was curious. "What will happen? How might I react? I can't say, but there's this: it's hardly conceivable that I won't discover something of importance—that I won't somehow solidify."

Marie-Christine did her best to reassure Mother by explaining that we were cognizant of the perils of young marriage but that after all we were not young by local standards and we knew one another very well indeed. The next day I managed to be alone with Mother—it was difficult—and I took much the same line. Also I told her I found it strange that she should have spoken to Marie-Christine the way she had. "It seemed to me you almost gave her a warning—why did you do that, Mother?" It was the closest I had ever come in my life to discussing my situation with her. She shrank into her chair and avoided looking at me for several awkward moments and then said, "I'm not sure, Victor. It's only that she's such a nice girl. . . ." Then she flushed violently, staring at me with wide appealing eyes.

It was clear that she was telling the truth—she *wasn't* sure. At last I was certain that for some twenty years she had been not merely subtle but also self-deluded—had looked away from the truth with the firmness of insanity. Of course this enormously saddened me for it proved that I was alone after all—I had been taking sustenance all that time from a purely imaginary sympathy and understanding. But what intrigued and even alarmed me was the fact that Mother's rigid madness seemed to be breaking up—she didn't yet know the truth, but she had felt its pressure. My understanding of these things gave me a tactical advantage of sorts.

Marie-Christine's state of mind was less clear to me. Of course she must have been in a general way aware that I was far from conventional. I sometimes toyed with the possibility that she might have an instinctive comprehension of the exact nature of my situation. I supposed it would be a shock forced suddenly on her consciousness, but I imagined her quite capable of absorbing such a shock. Nevertheless I thought that if the revelation must come it would be better when she and I were on our own away from the tensions of my home. Therefore my first thought was to smooth Mother's ruffled spirit. For a few days my placid demeanor, my solicitous attentions seemed successful, but soon her eyes told me this was insufficient.

After some thought I hit on a strategy of diversion. The general idea came to me in a flash—I was rehearsing to myself a conversation between Mother and Marie-Christine which I had overheard. They had been chatting about Marie-Christine's relatives, and she had described an uncle who, having demonstrated great flair for business, had disappointed the family by dying young. What now struck me was that the talk had then continued to meander: Mother had not seized the opportunity to lament the similar case of my father. As I thought about it I realized that scarcely a word had been said about him since we had been home. Furthermore, when I skimmed through the huge packet of letters Mother had written in the past four years I saw that after the first year there had been a decline in such observations as "your father would be proud," a decline so gradual that I had not even remarked the fourth year's lack of any mention of him. Poor Mother! I seized and played on this point of apparent weakness a little ruthlessly.

The next evening at dinner I turned the conversation once more to Marie-Christine's uncle. Mother said, "It must have been a terrible misfortune. I always have such sympathy for . . ." and then she stopped, staring at us wonderingly and foolishly in the candle-light. ". . . for such misfortunes," she went on. Marie-Christine said, "Do you feel unwell, Mrs. Barron?" "No, my dear."

I nourished the seed I had planted with scattered sentences—"Didn't this belong to my father?"—spacing them widely in the hope that I might play the thing out over the entire summer. Mother's reactions were marvelously various. Sometimes she snatched eagerly at the opening and tried to lead me into talk of my father; but then I would grow distant and uninterested. Sometimes she virtually flinched, and then I would press her a bit more. Marie-Christine said, "I think I see what you're up to, but are you sure it's the best way to help her? Aren't you upsetting her needlessly?" I said, "Anything worthwhile is bound to be painful."

Indeed the treatment proved more tonic than I expected or wished. One afternoon while Marie-Christine was napping I had been helping Mother with her gardening. We were resting on a little wrought-iron bench surrounded and partly shaded by the bean poles. Before I saw what was happening—before I could prevent it—Mother began to call my bluff. She was fanning herself, and out of the blue she said, "There's something, you know, that's been on my mind, and I've thought we ought to speak about it—in strictest honesty, Victor, that your father would have been—was—really a genius, strictly speaking, you know, *can't* be proved—since he never had a chance to prove it himself. Of course I had faith in him, but then a proper wife always does, and I think now that in the early years of my grief" (she actually used these words) "I may have exaggerated his promise. It's something I've realized clearly only in the last few days, Victor—I believe you've suspected something of the sort yourself, haven't you?—anyway I feel better now that we've straightened it out. I imagine you'll want to talk it over with Marie."

This surprised and shocked me—I certainly hadn't suspected it. I had tried to guess the reason for her uneasiness about my father, but this sort of thing had never entered my mind. Instinctively I thought, "She's lying," but I saw that she was not. She had been speaking rapidly and breezily, staring into space, but now that she looked at me I saw that if anything she had been softening and glossing over the whole truth. I could think of nothing to say—I could hardly think at all. For a moment I simply sat and watched her. She had dropped her fan. Among the soft bean leaves lacy with wormholes she seemed something in a mad dream, a middle-aged princess in a flurry of green valentines. I hurried away to be alone with myself.

When I had recovered my self-possession I decided that it behooved me to play my shock for all it was worth. It seemed bizarrely possible that what had been troubling Mother was just the necessity of making this revelation about my father. In any case I had to try to make her believe so. I thought it would be well to make Marie-Christine think so too. I did not need to dissimulate my own turmoil, I merely showed it. I returned home preserving a quiet dangerous demeanor. Mother and Marie-Christine had conferred, and they eyed me anxiously. Meanwhile back at the Kirkwood house I was beginning the first sections of this story. That night Marie-Christine comforted me. "You oughtn't take it so hard, and think of her—she's at her wit's end, she had no idea." I promised to do what I could. I was genuinely very depressed though. I must have paid little attention to anything but memories of my childhood, for now I find myself unable to recall much of the days immediately following Mother's revelation. I think she kept largely to her shop, and I know Marie-Christine did what she could to ease things for everyone.

The mathematician Gödel had recently done a rather spectacular proof of a new theorem. Roughly what it said was that any logical system generates comprehensible statements that can neither be proved nor disproved within that system. I felt as if my life had meandered into that sort of unevaluable statement. In the literature I knew, the closest thing to my state of mind seemed George Eliot's Baldassare, in whose anguish and senility the very meaning of language would flicker and vanish. Like that old man I needed revenge, it seemed. But even this idea was a disturbance always at the edge of my vision, impossible to focus.

It's more and more difficult to continue. Something of the feelings I had then keeps coming back to me—the feeling that it was all alike from beginning to end so that I don't need to know any more. I remember we were all extraordinarily quiet—in fact toward the end we hardly said anything—and yet then, and now, it felt like being in the center of a noisy argument, being caught in crossfire of loud senseless assertion, knowing it was going to keep going on without any agreement's being reached. And yet we grew quiet as mice toward the end.

The feeling of noise grew especially intense at times, like that when I came upon Mother braiding Marie-Christine's lovely hair in the grape arbor. It made me feel I had a hangover. Something had to be done. I returned to the Kirkwood house and talked it over. Something had to be done, otherwise it seemed Mother's madness might leave her to possess me. I felt like saying to Marie-Christine, "Hitler indeed! How can I think about him at a time like this?" Clearly we would have to leave, she and I, for our sakes, regardless of what it did to Mother. Anyway I had begun to fear that Mother's illness, her physical illness, whatever it was, was bogus. I hardly knew what to do other than leave. I found Marie-Christine and made love to her and told her my plans.

"Perhaps you're right after all," she said. "I don't like to say it, but when she was handling my hair I felt uneasy. I didn't enjoy having her touch me, I don't know why. But I won't have a scene, darling, not with her. I mean to say I'd sneak away some night rather than that."

At dinner she looked lovely and very happy. Mother said, "I hope Victor found some way to entertain you this afternoon my dear. You must be finding it tedious here. . . ." For a moment it looked like an opening, but then it began to look more like a lure or even a dare although Mother did look more sad than defiant. But I had started to talk and couldn't very well stop so that somehow these words came out: "You know, there must be comedies that are ugly through and through."

A few days passed. Mother seemed to be waiting. At last I said something like "Marie-Christine has to return to New York next week, and . . ."

"You've been a charming guest, my dear, and we shall certainly be sorry to see you go," etc. I let it pass for the moment, but the next day I told Mother I planned to go east for a while too. Timidly she said, "I don't think you ought to, Victor. I've been thinking, you know. . . ."

"Dear Mother," I said, and embraced her—she cowered like a kitten or a puppy in my arms—"you mustn't worry yourself about my plans. I've always appreciated your thoughtfulness, but you know I have to plan for myself now."

"Stay, Victor," she pleaded. "I'm worried. There's so much we should discuss. Things will work out, I'm sure they will." Unfortunately Marie-Christine entered in time to hear and misinterpret the last sentence. She said, "Oh, Victor, you've told her. I was afraid you wouldn't approve, Mrs. Barron. But this is lovely. You must start planning to come to New York for the wedding. I hardly have a family to speak of, but my cousins are there."

"I don't think I could travel so far," Mother said, and then she fainted.

"Poor dear," said Marie-Christine. "Well, then, we can have the wedding here I suppose." I felt like explaining nothing. We put Mother to bed. I left Marie-Christine to revive her, and I went to the Kirkwood house to think.

Only now does it occur to me to wonder what Mother said to Marie-Christine when she revived—at the time it hardly seemed to matter. I simply had to give up control, rest for a while, let happen what would. I believe it was toward evening, and raining. I think it was then I marked a quotation in a book I was reading, to be included in this story:

Die tollsten Fieberphantasien, die kuhnsten Erfindungen der Sage und der Dichter, welche Thiere reden, Gestirne stille stehen lassen, aus Steinen Menschen und aus Menschen Baume machen, und lehren, wie man sich am eignen Schopfe aus dem Sumpfe zieht, sie sind doch, sofern sie anschaulich bleiben, an die Axiome der Geometrie gebunden.

Then there were some days in which everyone felt gloomy and disgruntled and kept largely to himself, and when any of us spoke it was abruptly, out of the blue:

Marie-Christine: "Make her see I'm not as she supposes. Who does she think she is to tell me about wickedness?"

Mother: "I must forbid your marrying her, Victor, there's nothing else I can do. Victor, I have been a madwoman—how did you let me become so confused?"

Me to Mother: "I love and pity you and honor you, but you have given up your right. We'll leave soon, and you must reconcile yourself."

Marie-Christine: "I won't be alone with her, Victor."

Marie-Christine: "We must manage it without a scene, for my sake. I'm such a coward."

Me to Marie-Christine: "We can just get on a train and vanish. We're young."

The time seems broken with such remarks. Sometimes some of us mumbled so that we could scarcely be heard. When I was alone I called myself "we" for the first time. It proved easy and meaningless. I felt like something which is meant to shed light and does not.

There were ironies I scarcely noticed then but which please me more now that I think about them. Mother, taking drastic action to prevent the marriage she thought wrong, sought support from her friends among the townspeople. I heard about it from Roy Struthers, who with much hesitation told me he thought she needed "looking after" since she seemed to be "wandering." "Poor thing, she was insisting you had a twin brother and that I had to keep you from going off with that nice girl to get married. I humored her, I thought that would be best."

And so she herself provided the suggestion for what finally gave me a kind of trump card. She had grown absolutely determined. She even admitted what she had been up to: "I've talked to some people already, told them you shouldn't get married. You must know it's because I love you, Victor, and it's tearing me apart, but I know what I must do. If you leave I will follow you, I'll tell everyone on the train, I'll tell people in New York, I'll write to Harvard College, I owe it to you both, and to myself. . . ." She burst into tears. Marie-Christine said, "Ah Victor, but I can't have this. You must work it out with her. I'll leave in a few days, and then if you can work it out you come too." Of course she was a terrible coward, but it made me only love her the more. And so the next day I arranged to have Mother committed to a "rest home" in a town nearby. How she shrieked when they came for her! Roy Struthers did his best to quiet her. It was early in the morning—we thought it would be easier if she were drowsy. It was in fact the hour when I used to come creeping down or up the stairs. But the noise awakened Marie-Christine, and she insisted on finding out what was happening. "It's the best thing," I explained. "You can see she'd have brought it on herself eventually. She'll be well taken care of."

"I see," said Marie-Christine, very gravely. A few days later she was gone. I should never have let her out of my sight I suppose, but things seemed to have worked themselves out and I was exhausted. She said I had gone "really too far," and that she had to leave, I would not be able to locate her, perhaps the love would come back and she would write, perhaps not.

Furious and disgusted, I had Mother brought back home, but we could not bring ourselves to say much to one another. I suppose she had little energy left anyway. She proved to have been in bad health after all, and she died not long after. This is another of those old ironies: things really were working out unbeknownst to Marie-Christine and me. I suppose Mother felt she was dying and for that reason was especially frantic toward the end.

Now I want to quarrel a little with a certain sort of reader of my story. I know the world is full of people like Marie-Christine, inclined to make the sort of objections that rouse me to replies like, "How can you expect me to worry about Hitler at a time like this!" I mean that there are people who will suppose my story to be folly of the worst kind. I want to anticipate their objections by saying, "Folly's not so easy to pinpoint as all that, would that it were." I maintain that it's no good merely to explain things away because they can always sneak back. We ought to work through whatever comes to hand in good faith and not go flying off after something else just because nobody would call *that* folly.

First I ought to say that I've begun to suspect that the real problems and issues may be quite different from what I had supposed. Looking at things from this end alters the perspective. When interesting men play billiards one watches the table of course whether the play is good or bad or simple or intricate, and yet all the time it's only the game in the men's minds that's of any importance. So with Marie-Christine and me, except that even our emotions and opinions were like the billiard balls at play, and the important game is the retrospective one in my mind now. Surely the events matter less than what I think about them.

In a way the real question was whether things would be disastrous. If the story has a primary moral I think it must be this: avert catastrophe. Hold back, maintain the dispassionate eye when your life seems to lean out. In the Alps Antony for all his custom of luxury ate "strange flesh, which some did die to look on." We know so little that there is no point in drama and in particular none in catastrophe. The only final solution is an empty one like Hitler's suicide.

I can't say whether I'll see Marie-Christine again. I'm of a mind to remain here for some time, and it would certainly be convenient if she came back. When people ask after her I give them elaborate, varying, and contradictory lies to explain her absence. It's been a painful process, but I've finally learned that there is almost no limit to almost everyone's credulity. The other evening I went out for a walk together. Old Elias Leeper my neighbor saw me and promptly sat down on the sidewalk and began shaking his head and pounding on it with his fist. An automobile caught me in its headlights and careened wildly. I returned home, for the townspeople's safety.

Marie-Christine and I could live here comfortably whether or not I confronted her with the full truth of my situation. In fact I could see us settling down here in pastoral retreat, enjoying our subtleties, watching them grow outdated—perhaps we'd raise interesting children. Part of the point I want to make is that I'm unwilling to predict anything more than that things will continue for me in one intriguing form or another and that I shall continue to try to deal with them.

Another of the real issues of my story seems now to have been that of language. I write these words in a period which is seeing parallel movements in literature and philosophy—in both realms attention is turning toward *ordinary* language. These movements are being hailed as revolutionary, and doubtless they are. In any case my history has been that of an extraordinary being confined to ordinary language. It has enabled, even forced me to maintain the illusion that I am like other people. But this means that ordinary language has failed everyone else with respect to me—or has it? What shall I say here? The question is surely of the trustworthiness of ordinary language.

One further point also has to do with ordinariness. As I look back over what I have written I notice that in a way this has been the story of my peculiarity. But what I have known all along, and what I've finally learned to codify for myself, is that the ways I differ from other people are much less important—even much less noticeable—than the ways I'm like them. And I have made a resolution, which may be the major consequence of all the events I've described: I intend to *be more like other people* as much as possible, and this will surely be the great undertaking of my remaining life.

SEVEN POEMS

BRAM DIJKSTRA

MISS BRANDON AT EIGHTY-TWO

Light falls (grey) over bushes
pinpointed against the sky;

And old miss Brandon walks:

her dried-up haunches flaking
(spindled in the draughts of autumn)
while the rains of night
are caught against
the pawnshop window of her skin.

She walks:

pain on a leash
a lozenge
for your song

(a dollar in the trees)

days don't
hills don't

but women
to be sure
forever—

And slovenly
against a sky clipped
from a faded pattern
she works herself
along the street:

a fuzzy touch of blue
along a trailing fence.

NAIMA

(*Live at the Village Vanguard—Again*)

In these hours of morning
words are pale—
my longing will not furrow pain

as you do.

Standing here
a reed against my tongue
and time's own bread
skin tight
            around my
thought,
I breathe your love—

a curve of spiders
                        sung
in blues
            to pulling veins
            to you

don't let my squirreled head
push carts around your presence

go

my hands must find their way—so
leave me

music is touch
                    a flower
open
        as you do.

ENTERTAINING THE TROOPS

The barracks are
of wood and steel.

A television set stands (dead)
on a small platform
near the door.

Cheap plastic paneling
surrounds the men.

Slouched round
square tables (small: formica),
drinking beer,
they eye the go-go dancer—
see her twice (she's on
a platform backed by mirrors:
after all, she has a lot of men
to entertain).

Heels, fishnet tights
and a bare belly:
her body's hard—

molded and immobile
(though she moves).

Her breasts are hidden
by a tassled bra,
which, when she shakes,
gives visions of
colossal motion.

Her face
(all but the open oval
of her mouth)
has disappeared
in hair,

and as she moves,
her one hand seems to reach
for the TV set
near the door
(while the other
simply floats).

The men look on
in silence.

MALCOLM MALCOLM

Inside tall knowledge
all is still.

Hard current birds
leap time—brief messages of anger
touch forbidden sand.

Dark spots of soil remain
and tracks of skin
fade into eyes.

Strong tensile fingers mold
lice into stone:

Among the images of past disdain
burned forms of story
wriggle free.

Black is the sound of memory:

Words of a broken past
move silently
along the narrow streets of thought.

Though days of hatred claim
rude fragments of a man,
tall certain knowledge
cannot be destroyed:

It slices through despair
and breaks the frozen thighs
of whites too unconcerned to run.

THE ADVENTURES OF CAPTAIN INTELLECTUAL

A little village in the Styx
still burned
            when Billy passed it:

"Behold me, Bagmen!"
                    was his call
and with a stunning
                    zero
crashing from brick eyes
he
    (cloaked
            and dagger to the fore)

    took part
    when
         ripped the awning—

The stunning crack
clipped his left wing
but then

    the girl

and proffered him
bright succor!

Up flashed
and held her smiling:
a fire through his
as tender—

He swept the streets
and flames were dead
as
   with a sigh
no more his cloak
and cover to the world,

alone again,
he left
     (unhealed)
on both his meager crutches.

THE PHILOSOPHY OF LANGUAGE

words

are merely paper bags:
we pick up our pieces

wherever we find them
(candy counters, super-
market bakery shops)

and I know this:
we don't speak of ancient
civilizations—we
visit them in
each other's eyes.

Sometimes we even
touch another's

skin

A NOTE CONCERNING THE POETIC IMAGINATION

As she lifted
her skirt
he could see
the rental agreement
pinned to her crotch.

This made him curse
"the vicious circle
of the seasons
and the willow's
slumped down posture
fallow in
the early sunlight's
blinding rut"—

Poets are all the same:
They don't know a good
thing
when they see it.

POEMS BY POETS FROM AFRICA

ONYEGBULE C. UZOARU • OKOT p'BITEK •
CHINWEIZU • IFEANYI MENKITI • CHRISTOPHER
OKIGBO • KOFI AWOONOR

Edited by Ifeanyi Menkiti

ONYEGBULE C. UZOARU: TWO POEMS

FOR THE LADY IN CUBICLE B

the lady in cubicle B is a
nullip.
i am the doctor, m.d.
she is the lady, in labor.
it ain't no fun
sitting and waiting on nullips
in Braxton Hicks.
i got a c-section elsewhere
to oversee.

i try to slip by
her door
kept a quarter way open
by the compulsive chief nurse.

doctor! doctor!
see
you ain't gonna slip by me.
what are doctors for?

i walk into cubicle B
gently
eyes scanning the environment in its
entirety.
the monitor: early deceleration, good
variability . . . nothing to worry about.
Bedside records: good vital signs, normal
phase duration . . . good.
pelvic exam: as expected . . . couldn't
be better.

a quick look at her face
all i see is
labor pains. i feel like
crying
but i can't 'cause she gives me
a sign
she is full of joy
going through the best experience
of her life.

i guess i'm inexperienced
in telling
what mona lisa feels. but i know
the tension in those muscles.
i know
the vicious circle
of ferguson reflex.
i know
the bladder has joined the bowel
in a fight
against compression. look lady
i'm gonna cry
'cause i know more than you do.

it's friday night doc.
she says.
all i gotta do is
ball
with my baby. it ain't painful.
it's something else, got me?
you have the theory, doc. i
the feeling.

LONELINESS

i sit on the edge of life
not alone, but lonely.

the space is too crowded.
moths and worms all over,
creeping tender limbs
fat oval bodies
degenerative joints squeaking
with old age
it's a mixture of generations
not at war, but warring.

alone,
i had a partner . . .
loneliness.

now
the air is hot
and stuffy
faces all over
generations of hot sweat melting
down human icicles.
how far away is sahara desert?

give me a huge blanket.
i am cold.

OKOT P'BITEK: A POEM

MY HUSBAND'S HOUSE IS
A DARK FOREST OF BOOKS

Listen, my clansmen,
I cry over my husband
Whose head is lost.
Ocol has lost his head
In the forest of books.

When my husband
Was still wooing me
His eyes were still alive,
His ears were still unblocked,
Ocol had not yet become a fool
My friend was a man then!

He had not yet become a woman,
He was still a free man,
His heart was still his chief.

My husband was still a Black man
The son of the Bull
The son of Agik
The woman from Okol
Was still a man,
An Acoli.

*

My husband has read much.
He has read extensively and deeply,
He has read among white men
And he is clever like white men

And the reading
Has killed my man,

In the ways of his people
He has become
A stump. . . . .

•

O, my clansmen,
Let us all cry together!
Come,
Let us mourn the death of my husband,
The death of a Prince
The Ash that was produced
By a great Fire!
O, this homestead is utterly dead,
Close the gates
With *lacari* thorns,
For the Prince
The heir to the Stool is lost!
And all the young men
Have perished in the wilderness!

And the fame of this homestead
That once blazed like a wild fire
In a moonless night
Is now like the last breaths
Of a dying old man!

There is not one single true son left,
The entire village
Has fallen into the hands
Of war captives and slaves!
Perhaps one of our boys
Escaped with his life!
Perhaps he is hiding in the bush
Waiting for the sun to set!

But will he come
Before the next mourning?
Will he arrive in time?

Bile burns my inside!
I feel like vomiting!

For all our young men
Were finished in the forest,
Their manhood was finished
In the classrooms,
Their testicles
Were smashed
With large books!

CHINWEIZU: THREE POEMS

I'M NOT SHY

Hey ant!
Not here!
Please crawl out
Oh! You've stung my balls!
What an itch!
Come out!
Or do you want me to pull my pants down
Under this crowd's big eye?
Now, don't get me wrong.
I'm not shy.
The girls, I'm sure, will understand;
But what about those cops?

CULTIVATED MAN

They said he was a cultivated man,
And in my loose-tongued naïveté,
While others displayed awed respect,

I blurted out
An unconsidered question:
    Cultivated with what plow,
    Sowed with what seed
    Tended with what care,
    And fruitful with what?
I drew scorching looks of scorn!

THE SAVIOR

He arrived and went straight to the city fathers and declared:
"I've come to die for your sins."
The surprised fathers looked at him and said:
"We have no sins!"
"How can that be?" he answered them. "Don't you drink,
    or smoke or cuss? Don't you rob?"
"We do that every day; what else is there to do?"
"Well then! I've come to die for your sins."
"Very well," said the elders. "But first, sit among us and eat
    and drink with us."
But when he would neither eat nor drink with them, nor sit
    among them, nor go away, and had bored and irritated them
    with incessant talk about his mission, they ordered him to
    be taken out beyond the city gates and crucified.
It was done.

IFEANYI MENKITI: SEVEN POEMS

CANTEMUS, THEREFORE

where the saints
in glory stand
around

the high throne
of heaven's God—

an expert on the life of Bologna
in the fifteenth century;
the son of a tribal chief
recruited by the missionaries;

cantemus, therefore,
to the Lord
God of hosts.
He has carried
with us
our several griefs.

GENE STUFF

Today I learn
that they have just
discovered
the substance
that turns on the genes
telling, for instance,
the nose genes
that the nose
is about to be made
and turning off,
therefore,
the toe genes
finger genes
and the rest,
so as to preserve
the pure form
of the nose
and, as it were,
not end up
with a mess

part toe & part nose,
a toe-nose, so to speak;
and I say to myself
how smart the body is:
much smarter
than the tribe
of philosophers
& the transcendence
that sings in their heads.

WHAT THOU LOVEST WELL

And anyone, who has
ever had

a brilliant disease

would know what
the poet meant to say

when he said
that the mind shines

only with suitable agitation;

to pluck excellence
from the virulence
sown

by determined
little organisms
feeding on the psyche;

that Sylvia ended it
& Berryman, also,
could not hack it;

where my song fades
westward with the wind;

a suitable night
to connect with this sorrow;

an old man on whom
the sun has gone down,

for whom the inward light
did not always cohere.

CLEAR SONG BEFORE THE MASK

three diagonal
slits
on the mask's face;
the burden
of the ancestors
brought home this day;

and to attend to this
is not to concede
Senghor his point
but to acknowledge
Onitsha
the spirits that move her.

ADAIBA

The clear stream in the clear day
shall flow with her return;
and may the glow escort her,

as I rise to meet her;
the deep one gird with god-light.

AGE OF THE GODS WHO NEVER CAME

Age of the gods who never came,
the rose calling, hinting, never blooming;
in season, out of season,
trailing the secret hours:
Son of man, son of man . . .

Singer, in the dark fields,
what means this burning of darkness?
and what this motion of closed years?
this projection through time in still dance?
what mean?

Son of Man,
the kingdom of God is within you;
the kingdom of God is also moving
onward and upward, in stillness,
                              into stillness.

And water also will burn;
nor will I be not willing
            to tell of this
when my song of flame is ended—

Who moved among the astral marshes,
tongue-tied, still chanting in the night.

ALL QUIET ON SLAVE ROW

            Nor could they tell
            whether the Negro

was of man
or was somewhere
between an antelope
and a man.

•   •

We danced on the ephemera
the ephemera danced with us;
us and the ephemera were one.

Lord of joy
and intermingled blessedness

Jerusalem was builded there
among the dark-set sea.

Arabs came,
the Jews before them;

but, here, in our authentic
southern sea, we wept

and spat the seeds
of watermelon—

jolly niggers
come to town.

And there was this adult pain
down deep in the soul

because of which
was laughter.

Lord of tears
and perspiratory blessedness

we shook, we shook
to the rhythm of juba.

CHRISTOPHER OKIGBO: A POEM

COME THUNDER

Now that the triumphant march has entered the last street corners,
Remember, O dancers, the thunder among the clouds . . .

Now that laughter, broken in two, hangs tremulous between the
    teeth,
Remember, O dancers, the lightning beyond the earth . . .

The smell of blood already floats in the lavender-mist of the
    afternoon.
The death sentence lies in ambush along the corridors of power;
And a great fearful thing already tugs at the cables of the open air,
A nebula immense and immeasurable, a night of deep waters—
An iron dream unnamed and unprintable, a path of stone.

The drowsy heads of the pods in barren farmlands witness it,
The homesteads abandoned in this century's brush fire witness it:
The myriad eyes of deserted corncobs in burning barns witness it:
Magic birds with the miracle of lightning flash on their feathers . . .

The arrows of God tremble at the gates of light,
The drums of curfew pander to a dance of death;

And the secret thing in its heaving
Threatens with iron mask
The last lighted torch of the century . . .

KOFI AWOONOR: *FROM* THE WAYFARER COMES HOME

IV *Echoes*

Wayfarer, alone now
upon the road,
rest now near the copse
near the cleavage in the hill
for rest calls you now.
   Stop awhile on the journey home
Your soul waits on the trail
of hunters, in the wake of harvesters.
What wearies your body
at this subliminal hour?
Come near the circular fire,
in this strange village
they will give you to eat
   and water your tired feet.
Though strangers, wayfarer,
   they understand the thirst
      in your throat, the hunger and fire
   in your belly
Let your cripple's crawl
   change into a warrior's gait
and dance the ancient dance of notables
The land your lover
   waits for you
its valleys greeny in September
its mountains blue beyond heaven.
She waits trailing her marriage gown
white, her headgear indigo
her necklace of precious beads
in a circlet of red.
She stands out there
   on the outskirts of a native village
      crying softly for joy

She stands out there

in the midst of old glories
waiting for your homecoming

Wayfarer, you who knows
the shape of every rock on this mountain,
the texture of every leaf in this valley,
You who have measured with your tears
    every weary mile.

Your companions are the sparrow's aunt
the eagle's father
and the wild cock's concubine
You have shared a laugh with the hyena
a handshake with the monkey
and hooted back at the deep-eyed owl at dusk.
Every blade of grass knows the weight
    of your footfall, every wind
        the smell of your sweat
Come now, hurry home
follow the echo of your natal sounds
follow the call of the wren
and the evening bell cry of the pigeon dove.
Hurry on home, wayfarer
leave the sooty cities of the evil animal.

I have learnt to listen to the evening
to sit quietly by my bed of mercy
    waiting for you to come home.
I have learnt to count evening shadows
at noon, to signify the enormity of my fate
in the enclosure of my hands.
In the rains yesterday
I wished to dance again
the dance I did in youth
I wished for the sun this September day
to embrace the old slaves my comrades of this fort
whose ghosts torment my sleep.
In solitary I brood over the cats
and the flowers outside
I count the iron bars in the overhead cage

The flowers weep, wayfarer
Come home now to the mountain
Come to the greeny valley
Come dance with me
   at our jubilee; Laugh again
Your ancient laugh. You know
our gods are maimed
by native and foreign cudgels
muffled yet stout their voices remain
to proclaim the festival
of your homecoming.

Here, in this brief corridor of desolation
in this concrete yardage of pain
we snatch little joys in remembrance
of a place once where the baby lay
of the pleasure at the mourner's ululation.
Here the tumult has barely died down
where the sun proclaimed a respite
  symbolic gestures of a tired man
   revealed now as
    great truths and visions
     long known, terrible presentiments
      shrinking with tidal turns, reckonings.

I pause for breath, wayfarer
I pause for a brief benediction.

V *One Alone: The Bird Sweeps*

At the first journey, at dawn
the sea emerges. Some call her mad
She yields to the land of pure sand
beautiful beyond recalling.
On clear days, the eye
can sweep across the old plantation
maintained once by slave labor
its harvest long buried in history

the grandeur of this land
defies poetry and music
But they still sing of her
in long voluminous poems
in elaborate symphonies
There is rhythm of course
as you cannot talk
of this land without rhythm. . . . .

I love you, I love you
tatters and all. I shield you
with my pain.
I seek release from diseases
so I can bring you cure.
Take away this fatigue of the soul,
send a message to Soweto
on my behalf.
Tell them the festival time is come
that the heap slags of the raw cities
will burn,
that the dance has begun
the drummers all in place;
this dreary half life is over
our dream will be born at noon.
The night is for plots and strategems.
We shall harness the flames for the revolt
pride shall lead us into armories

We shall stalk the evil animal
    a hundred years times ten hundred
    even beyond the moon.
We abjure all malice
We claim the sanctity of the ambush
    and clean revenge.
We love the smell of dead animals.

In this hour before victory
trace me every line on the dragonfly
count me the legs of the spider hen

the various tongues of water
   and the crisscross of the wind.

Tell me how often the baboon fornicates
how frequent the mountains breathe.
The fish says I know his hiding place
Already the gull's island is my treasure store
Gemi and Amu, mountain and river
shift the stress upon my heart.

So I make this journey now;
there will be no detours
I shall live on rawhide and locusts
I shall drink of the only wine you serve
   and in the ugly hour long ordained
I shall grind my knife.

I will have no trophies to show
For the swamp beneath the hills
   shall receive the evil animal.

                              Ussher Fort Prison
                        September 17–22, 1976

BIOGRAPHICAL NOTES

ONYEGBULE C. UZOARU is from Nigeria. He received a bachelor's degree in chemistry from Columbia University and holds an M.D. degree from the University of Pennsylvania School of Medicine. He is presently associated with St. Luke's Hospital, Bethlehem, Pa. His poems have appeared in *Nimrod* and in the volume *Poets and Authors* published by Harlow (Detroit).

OKOT P'BITEK was born in Gulu, Uganda. He studied law at Aberystwyth and social anthropology at Oxford. His Lwo novel *Lak Tar* was published in 1953. In addition to the *Song of Lawino,* from which the selection included here is reprinted, he has also published *Song of Ocol* and *Song of a Prisoner.* He is presently a lecturer at the University of Nairobi, Kenya.

CHINWEIZU, author of the historical study *The West and the Rest of Us* and the book of verse *Energy Crisis and Other Poems,* is presently associate editor of the African literary magazine *Okike.* His essays, poems, and polemics have appeared in *Presence Africaine, The American Poetry Review,* and the *Times Literary Supplement.* He was educated at Government College, Afikpo, Nigeria, and in the United States at M.I.T. and the State University of New York at Buffalo.

IFEANYI MENKITI is the author of two books of poems, *Affirmations* and *The Jubilation of Falling Bodies.* His third collection, *Without Loss of Temper,* is scheduled for publication in 1979. Other of his poems have appeared in the *Pan African Journal, Evergreen Review, Sewanee Review,* and *New Letters.* He studied at Christ the King College, Onitsha, Nigeria, and later at Columbia and Harvard universities. He has been a recipient of awards in poetry from the Massachusetts Arts and Humanities Foundation (1975) and from the National Endowment for the Arts (1978). Presently he teaches philosophy at Wellesley College.

CHRISTOPHER OKIGBO (1932–67), was killed in action in 1967 while fighting on the Biafran side during the Nigerian civil war. His publications include *Heavensgate, Limits, Silences,* and the posthumous collection *Labyrinths.* The selection reprinted here is from "The Path of Thunder" sequence of *Labyrinths.* In the sequence the poet clearly foresaw and came to prophesy the forthcoming civil war that was to take his life.

KOFI AWOONOR has published these volumes of poetry: *Night of My Blood, Ride Me Memory, The House By the Sea,* and *This Earth My Brother.* He was born in Ghana and holds degrees from the University of London and the State University of New York. He taught for several years at SUNY at Stony Brook and on going back to Ghana was arrested and imprisoned for allegedly trying to overthrow the government. He was held at Ussher Fort Prison, and *The House By the Sea,* from which the selection included here is reprinted, is a result of that experience.

TWINS

CHRISTINE L. HEWITT

Your sister wrote exactly five suicide notes. Stylistically, they moved from florid (almost comic) overstatement into a simplicity that was so straight and easy to pronounce that you were finally reminded of an old American barn, its only decoration a golden weather vane, a rooster.

Delia was very tall. No shelf in the kitchen, stocked with exotic canned goods, was too high for her. She had short blonde hair and eyes like buttonholes. The color of her eyes was dark brown, although many people found that hard to imagine. Long dark lashes fluttered nervously at the edges of her eyelids. Her mouth was almost always painted fire-engine red. For formal occasions, she would outline her lips in black with an eyebrow pencil. (There were less and less formal occasions.) She was very exact; she would not tolerate the tiniest smudge. Delia had a sharp chin. Sometimes it seemed to be pointing at what she wished her eyes would focus upon. But while her chin was pointing at the ducks, mating at the far end of the pond, Delia's eyes were focusing on the clouds.

The neighbors thought that Delia wore the same clothes all the time. This was not so. She had many pairs of corduroy pants, many tee shirts with animals silk-screened on them, and many sweatshirts with hoods. It's true that they all looked alike, if one was not used to distinguishing between the pair with the faded bottom and the

114

pair with the frayed cuffs; or between a kangaroo on a pale blue background and a marmoset in a jungle setting. You, however, were used to distinguishing. Delia had only one pair of rubber boots. They were fire-engine red. Delia used to wear grey silk underwear beneath her corduroy pants and tee shirts: bikini pants and size 34B brassieres. Later, she didn't wear any underwear at all.

Your husband, Victor Delaroche, told her—when she first eschewed underwear—that her breasts would sag down to her navel and get in the way when she was canoeing or love-making. But Delia got her exercise, and proved him wrong. Her nipples stayed upright, and her body was no longer striped by the indentations of underwear elastic.

There is no need to describe you, physically, because you look exactly like your twin sister. Except that your eyelashes are short and as blonde as your hair. Your taste in clothes is where the difference lies, apparently. Turtleneck sweaters in every shade of black and silk flowers and skirts with sashes are your favorites. All your footwear is rubber or plastic. But your outfits will be gone into later. It should be pointed out that you and Delia both tended to have many versions of the same thing.

When your parents died in the same week, the same day, the same hour, you and Delia suffered an identity crisis. All previous education was brought to bear upon an analysis of orphanhood. Although you were too old to be legally orphaned.

Delia sat on the Sheraton chair in the living room, her legs crossed. She always sat in the Sheraton chair, so as to avoid looking at it. She said, "Everywhere I look, I recognize grief. Grief: a very well-dressed emotion. And sometimes, I lose it. It hides in cabinets. Then I have to seek it out."

You said, "When you find it next time, talk to it. Do more than recognize it. It won't be able to hide after that." You were lying down on the wall-to-wall carpeting. Your mother's pearls slid down the inclined plane between your chest and your neck, and nuzzled up to the black turtleneck. The brass chandelier was not turned on, and it was past twilight.

Delia said, "You always know what to do."

"Just for you. Not for anyone else," you said.

Victor's sportscar could be heard in the driveway. You had asked him to get a new muffler for the funeral. (This was before you were married.) He had tried, but it was hard to get parts for his model, a semicustom job.

It wasn't just during that short period of mourning, it was always, that you and Delia experienced a confusion of memory. Because memory is so visual, you could both picture the scene exactly and still not know who was playing what part. Who was skinny until puberty? Which one went through a chubby phase? Who fell through the thin ice into the algal pond and tried to save herself by grabbing her sister's ankle, a fragile support at best? Who set off firecrackers inside teacups? Who was born first? (The nurses pretended not to remember. The obstetrician absconded to Costa Rica.) And the last to lose a maidenhead? One of you was deflowered by Uncle Aralian, and it will never be certain which it was. You were both fourteen at the time. Aralian, your mother's youngest brother, was no child molester, but a shy young man awed into protracted muteness by the lust he felt for one of his nieces. (Perhaps he, too, didn't know which.) That one would let him fondle her, upright, pressed against an apple tree that bore wormy fruit; and she always knew that her sister was watching, graphing the path of his nervous hands, recording the time it took, pinpointing the exact spot where sex took place, and marking it down upon the architectural blueprints of the house and grounds. You and Delia have always had this fetish for getting everything down on paper; and you both persisted, even through the paper shortage, the ink-mixers' strike, the international lead crisis.

Your mother used to say to your twin selves—your pockets were stuffed with early drafts—"You'll burn it all when you get older, and saner."

Delia would answer, bravely, "Oh, just throw it all onto the pyre, when the time comes."

She turned to you, "Well, Stacey, what do *you* think? Where did Delia learn about pyres? Has she been at the encyclopedia again?" She smiled unexpectedly; she didn't expect you to answer. She was wearing a long brown wool dress with a starched white collar. Because of those outfits, the first time you saw a picture of a nun you were confused.

It was early morning when Victor told you that he planned to marry you. The ducks could be heard quacking raucously, mocking the humans across the street, as always. Victor had spent the night with you, for the first time ever. You had put satin sheets on the bed. They were slippery, and you kept sliding onto the floor, and sometimes, rolling under the bed where you discovered a colony of dust.

Victor said, "We'll get married, but you have to know that I'll probably end up liking Delia as much as you."

"You mean, as much as I like her? I don't necessarily like her. I love her."

"No. As much as I like you."

"Remember, I'm the sane one. I'm the one who'll make a good mother."

"It's enough to drive someone crazy, the way you two look alike."

The plan was for the marriage ceremony to take place on the lawn beside the barn. Nine persons, and all their pets, were invited. Delia brought out the old architectural plans and pointed out that you could take your vows beneath the same tree against which *one of you* and Uncle Aralian had copulated, seven years ago. It became a moot point. A late summer hurricane arrived—on schedule, so said the guests—and you all removed to the barn. The guests were visibly fascinated by the collection of antique gardening tools. Your father, who had never caused anything to grow, had treasured them. His old law partner, George Sleaves, recognized one rusted three-pronged something or other.

George said, "This was on his desk beside the family pictures and the leaky inkwell. It stayed there until they crated up everything for posterity."

Delia laughed. A high-pitched laugh that was, mercifully, softened by the downpour. "Ah, posterity! That's us, Stace."

Many bottles of champagne had been chilled for the occasion, but the guests insisted on making cider in the old cider press instead. The hurricane tuned up its instruments out of doors, and the rain began to flood the barn. The old wooden floor became spongy. Everyone put on yellow rubber boots, except Delia, who wore her red ones. The way Victor kept bumping into Delia's chest, as they sloshed around in the rising water, was surely accidental. Your soggy pink-and-black wedding dress clung to your body and outlined the crack of your bottom.

George Sleaves ignored the activity surrounding the cider press, and went off to a corner to drink champagne, between a rusted manual lawnmower and a newer one. He popped the cork in your direction, and it barely missed elongating and widening your eye socket. George mouthed profuse apologies to you, as if the din in the barn was more than he could ever hope to overcome.

Everyone left when the sun came out. Water droplets on sagging leaves were outlined with yellow light. Victor took your elbow and steered you toward the house. He said, "It's true that kangaroos are dry-weather animals. But that's not true for all marsupials. The pouch, or marsupium, from which the group takes its name, is a flap of skin covering the nipples. I used to think this could be compared to the foreskin of a penis, but I have been told otherwise. Marsupials have an evolutionary memory of their own. Nonetheless, structural and behavioral parallels with placental mammals are in some cases striking. Such resemblances are examples of convergent evolution, a tendency for organisms to adapt in similar ways to similar habitats. Thus, there are marsupials that look remarkably like moles, shrews, squirrels, and marmosets."

"What has that got to do with the storm?" you asked.

Then you both heard Delia in the barn, throwing garden tools at the cider press. You ran back and watched her through a window. She was either laughing or shrieking. It did not surprise you to have that sort of confusion, not with Delia. When all the tools had been hurled—very little damage had been sustained, a nick here, a fleck of rust there—she gathered them all together and hung them back on the wall. It occurred to you that she would start all over again, but she sat down with some of the champagne George Sleaves had left behind.

Whatever she did, Delia had a way all her own of not giving the reason. It was a point of principle with her. Instead, she would offer descriptive passages, and self-mockery.

So when the time came for her to write suicide notes, she was un-equipped to explain her desire to quit this earthly life.

Do you remember the first? You remember the first as well as the second or the fifth, which is to say, they are all committed to memory, as indelibly as your shared birthday.

She had spent the day alone in her room, smashing bottles against the door. Perfume seeped through the threshold. Walking down the hallway, you expected to see stray sequins nestled in the cracks between the floorboards. You and Victor were engaged in a backgammon tournament, with each other. There were moments when the house itself must have shuddered, between the bottles being smashed upstairs, and the red and white playing pieces falling to the floor downstairs.

Toward dusk, Delia slit her wrists with one of the broken bottles. *As had to happen,* you thought all that night long. By the next morning, though, you were able to question the nature of the inevitable.

You had gone upstairs when the sound of smashing stopped. The neatly folded note beside her pillow read: "Stacey: Don't think this is a new idea. Not for me, not for anyone. It's historically valid. (What are encyclopedias for?) It has existed as a possibility for me ever since that day, when we were ten, and you overturned my inflatable duck and me in granny's pool. Instead of resisting, I sank slowly to the bottom, and when I looked up I could see your fat bottom and your baggy bathing suit. We, of course, were wearing identical bathing suits, and I can assure you, it was an eerie feeling. Certain things have always intrigued me, and one of them is the difference between being dead and being alive. But what can be the point of musing over that when one is only alive? It is my theory that one of two things will happen: Either, when I die you will know everything I ever knew; or, you will lose half your memories— you will not miss them, it will be as if they never existed. Either way, you will not know the difference. It will be as if there was only one of us in that womb. Remember? We thought we would be that warm for all time. We were so pleased with ourselves. Oh Stace! Writing this makes me feel so . . . permanent. To get on with it. I am not slitting my wrists because Sam Barnes, my childhood sweetheart, was just gunned down by mobsters in Chicago; but not before he could dash off a letter to me, terminating our relationship—what little was left of it—on account of his wife and three children in the suburbs. (He asked if you and I could still fit into each other's underwear. As if I would ever tell him!) Nor am I killing myself because our parents died and left us equal shares of everything. (But I am troubled that, after their death, we discontinued the use of all pet names. I have always considered it wise to establish some sort of secret name. It could be used as a signal, if one was ever forced by one's kidnappers to write a message, or for recognition after death.) As for technical failures, natural disasters, and broken bones: they don't seem to me sufficient reasons. Nor am I doing this because so much of our lives is a mystery: Mother's short career as a dancer in Panama; Father's manuscript on the Evolution of Rust; our Siamese aunts whose photo was lost in a windstorm. Did any of that ever bother you? Not me. I accepted what was unknowable in life. So now that you have read this, what more do you know than before? Remember how, before puberty, we turned the Process of Elimination into an exact science? I could go on in this vein ad nauseam, and alternately, I can't bear to write another word."

The time it took for you to read that note was enough time for a weaker person to have died in. The wrists you held gingerly in your hands were as fragile as dried and bleached sea urchins, as empty. They were the same size as your own wrists. As you applied the tourniquet to both upper arms, you could hear Victor pushing his feet into his rubber boots, and then letting the kitchen door slam behind him. From Delia's window, you could see him in the backyard, standing. It occurred to you that he had an ear cocked, that he was listening for the underground rumbling. When the doctor arrived, he immediately removed the tightly drawn string, to forestall the possibility of permanent damage to the nerves. But he complimented your knotwork: no slippage. That gratified you in a small way, and you noticed how handsome the doctor was, what taut thighs he had. Delia was unconscious, and he explained that now that the danger had passed, it was better that she remain that way, recollecting her strength.

It wasn't until after you were married that you learned that Victor spoke French: a little French; some French; a few choice words. It surprised you, because you were used to hearing only the hysteria of the ducks in the morning (and sometimes, Delia's dreamsongs). The flock had grown a third in size since the last season; this seemed portentous and wonderful to you. You loved the white-and-brown feathers that cluttered the shore and danced little duets with the gusts of wind. With Victor, you slept on sheets striped red and purple. Two of the four posters were truncated. There was sawdust on the floor. Victor said it "deafened the roar." You did notice that the puffballs of dust beneath the bed had disappeared. The mirrors in the bedroom faced each other, not the participants. One morning, Victor said, "Tu veux faire l'amour? Mon choux-fleur, ma jonquille tellement grande. Tiens toi droite. Ne bouge pas. Fais comme je te dis."

"Yes, yes, yes," was all you had to say.

Then afterward, you said, "If we had a child, you could teach her French. I'd like my children to be linguists." You fluttered your tongue against the back of your top front teeth, like a baby discovering its body, or like a leaf in the twilight of a windstorm.

"French doesn't leave the bedroom. So you understand?" said Victor.

"Yes, yes, yes."

In your mind, there is a special significance to Delia's second attempt to do herself in. The significance lies in having failed—if failed can be the word—once, and trying again. In one sense, it becomes the negation of all she might have learned; in another, it is the affirmation of that principle you argued over, as adolescents, by the edge of granny's pool, that of the Second Chance. Delia had said, "And what about the Last Chance Saloon? Existentialism? Nuclear Fallout? What about the San Andreas Fault?" "What about them?" you would reply, but you were probably underwater by then.

Delia's second try took place in the kitchen. It was unseasonably warm weather that day. You were making zabaglione, one failed batch after another. Delia was using the biggest ceramic mixing bowl. She stood bottles of detergents and cleaners up on the counter, and poured arbitrary amounts into her bowl. She hugged the bowl to her breasts as she blended the ingredients with a wooden spoon.

Curiosity came late in that sunny kitchen.

"What are you doing, Delia?" you asked. "Maybe it's the secret element missing from my zabag?"

"I'm inventing the ultimate cleaner. Once something is cleaned with this, it will be clean forever. I'm going to patent it under the name *Magic*."

It seemed like a good idea—the need for which no one would argue—so you left Delia alone with her inspiration and went down the road to foist some of your failed batched on your neighbors' pets, and one lone raccoon, a terrorist.

Delia was supine on the kitchen table when you returned, her hands folded atop her giraffe tee shirt. Her corduroy pants seemed shorter than usual—her ankle bones were clearly visible beneath her skin. Her teeth were as grey as your mother's Persian lamb coat. They clattered. That was the only sound in the sunny kitchen, with its foliage, its labor-saving devices, its clean smell.

You called the doctor. Over the telephone, it sounded as if his mouth was full. You pictured him sucking on those same lollipops he had given you and Delia as children, sick children, of course.

Delia's skin seemed translucent, and beneath it her veins were as blue as the Dutch pottery on the white kitchen walls. Her fingernails reflected like mica. Some eyelashes fell off and littered her cheeks like feathers on the opposite shore. You thought you knew what she meant by an "eerie feeling."

Then her eyes began to water; you were afraid she would use up the tears of a lifetime. Her veiny, boney hands sprang up to her eyes. You held them tightly by the wrists.

"Sorry, Delia, you can't touch them. And besides, crying isn't the worst thing you could be doing."

Her outpouring eyes ceased to preoccupy her when she started to retch. She leaned over and retched onto your sneakered feet. You brought her a bucket.

Then the doctor came, and he took the handle of the bucket from your hands. He looked all around the room and kept nodding his head.

"Aren't you going to pump her stomach out?" you demanded, and pointed to all the empty bottles that were rolling and resting on the linoleum floor.

"There'll be nothing to pump out when she's through," he said. "Did she really think this junk would make her do anything besides vomit?"

"You know that I believe in her intentions, I always have. But we didn't discuss them this time."

The doctor stayed until Delia had emptied herself out, and then he gave her a sedative. When you let him out the kitchen door he said, "Call me anytime," which seemed slightly perverse to you, given the circumstances. But then you noticed how handsome he was. And he had a smooth, silent sportscar.

It was a week later—the weather had taken a turn for the worse; godlike hissing could be heard in distant clouds—when you found

Delia's note, in the cabinet where all the detergents and cleaners used to be stored. "Stace. There is an inevitability to all this that baffles even me. I had to try again; and failed attempts don't seem to discourage me. Something I don't recognize is making me do this. I look forward to recognizing it. And you, you must understand how I anticipate discovering what lies on the other side of the abyss. When you finally read this, I will know whether it is harps or lyres the angels strum; whether their wings are attached to their flowing gowns or their celestial bodies; whether they can fly at will, or only when God sends them on an errand. My lullaby will be the music of the spheres, my breakfast will be the manna I collect from my cloudy pillow. Ambrosia will gush from heavenly fountains, and I will lap it up. Do you remember all the times we debated the sex of God? Not that we ever disagreed. As I write this I have the clearest picture in my mind: I expect that I shall find not exactly a hermaphrodite and not exactly a neuter, but someone with skin as soft and cold as snow, and hair as fine and fragile as the tentacles of a Portuguese man-o'-war, and the facial characteristics of a young boy who plays the ladies' parts in Elizabethan dramas. You may ask how I can know all this, now, and I can only suggest that proximity to the Pearly Gates has opened some doors in my head so that I can see what was always there."

You wanted to tease Delia about the whimsical nature of her latest note, and let her know how little it would have satisfied had she really died. But finally you didn't even tell her you had found it. You told Victor nothing, as usual. Delia replaced you as his backgammon partner in the evenings. You would look in on them sometimes and never know who was winning. Neither Victor nor Delia displayed any competitive instincts. You took up smoking cigarettes, long thin cigarettes, cigarettes in colored paper, hand-rolled cigarettes with strawberry flavor. You knew it would be a long time before you filled every ashtray in the house.

Sometimes Victor liked to lean out of bed and play with a handful of sawdust. You held his ankles for him. One night he told you that he had experimented with LSD, in the not so distant past.

"I loved to watch the birds when I was tripping," he said. "Only later did I learn that great auks were not evolutionary throwbacks; although they are now extinct. The last egg of the last great auk was thrown away by a Norwegian perfectionist because it had a tiny crack in it. Stacey! Are you listening?"

You were listening. You thought you heard laughter coming from Delia's room. But you couldn't be sure. Victor continued, "When I was tripping, I recognized the tunes the birds sang. I'd climb up on a branch, and we'd sing together. Different songs indicate different seasons. It's not what the ornithologists think at all."

"What about chromosome damage? Didn't that worry you?"

He covered your mouth with a pillow and crooned in French. Birds flew out the window.

Delia's third note was written in ink, and was unreadable by the time you got to it. She had left it on the sill of her bedroom window before throwing herself into the topiary garden. Perhaps she jumped repeatedly, only to bounce back. That is what occurred to you. (The shrubbery animals were shaggy by then. Your mother had imported Central American gardeners to do the original sculpting according to her specifications. Thus, the giraffe was humped and the kangaroo stood on all fours and the elephant had spindly legs, and so on.) Delia was too resilient. There was no way you could know if her fall was broken by the back of a vegetable mutation, but when you found her she was asleep between the webbed feet of a giant rooster. It was a moonful night. Victor was asleep and did not even dream of the lawn being pummeled. You came home late from partying. Was someone with you as you wandered through the darkened rooms and out the back door? Or did a sportscar leave you at the end of the driveway, and lurch into the night to the accompaniment of the ducks across the road? (Is any of that a good enough reason for the guilt you carry so close to you, that you want to envelope, marsupial-like?) She looked like your own ghost in the light of the moon. You brought her inside to bed; the arm that sagged around your shoulder was already wet with dew. Then the clouds broke, and it rained for days. So the ink ran across her note. But you could tell that this one was shorter than the others.

You dreamt of waking up to discover snow in the garden. But the brown leaves were still there, and the flower blossoms still dead upon their stalks—all those little broken necks. The weathervane spun atop the barn like a ride at an amusement park. The phone was ringing, and you didn't know what time it was. Victor was gone. It was George Sleaves on the phone.

"Good morning, Stacey. This is Stacey, isn't it?"

"Yes. It's me."

"You sound surprised to hear from me."

"I do? You can tell all that from three words?" Then you could hear him speaking to someone else. You pictured the manicured fingernails of his secretary.

George cleared his throat. "I called because it's time for you to sign some trust papers, and the new will. Delia's still stands, but yours should be changed since you've gotten married."

"But I haven't changed my mind about anything. Almost."

"You're not going to be difficult about it. It's a mere formality," he said. It was clear that something amused him.

"I promise to come in soon. Very soon. But I'm busy now, with animals. Good-bye." You set the receiver down very slowly; it was important that he realize just how carefully you had done it. Just how much could the wires transmit?

It was while drinking sparkling burgundy to celebrate your anniversary that Victor mentioned he was sexually attracted to your sister.

"Why her and not me? Why not both of us at the same time?" you asked, but not seriously.

"I have to wonder about that myself. Wonder whether it's the similarity or the difference that I want. I never confuse you two from a distance, but when you're side by side, I often feel uneasy."

"We don't. We're happy then." You lit a long thin cigarette and held it beneath your open hand, so that the smoke drifted up through the fingers.

Victor said, "There's something I learned recently that might interest you. The larger marsupials especially, embody nervous alertness and dull-witted consternation at the same time. A typical response of a red kangaroo when startled is to bound off in full flight—up to thirty m.p.h.—for a relatively short distance, stop short to reconnoiter the disturbance, and in what appears to be sheer panic, double back toward the adversary and jump over it."

You tapped at the cigarette with your index finger. "What's the difference between *what appears to be sheer panic* and *sheer panic*?"

"See? I knew this would interest you. Delia feels so differently about the animals. But as I say, I am so attracted to her."

"If you want to put it that way. And I've always been attracted to George Sleaves. If I don't do something about it soon, I may lose my chance." Until that moment, Victor had no inkling of your penchant for older men in respectable professions. That is not to say that he perceived it completely at that moment. But you were explicit. The next week you were awoken in the middle of a moonless night by an absence in your own bed, and uproarious laughter coming from Delia's room.

You were attached to your husband in different ways. First there was the trail of sawdust all through the house, and then there were your matching rhinestone-studded belts. None of this was necessary once he started sleeping with Delia. Then, the sound of his feet, padding along the hallway in their Turkish socks, became enough.

The first time you awoke in that absence, in the moist dawn, you did not go out to smoke in the barn. Rather, you listened to them with ears like tissue paper. The quacking of the ducks was a constant, so you had to learn to separate the strands of the different sounds. Delia had a beautiful voice. Victor seemed to be speaking to her in a Slavic tongue. Just once, you sat in the cold hallway and listened at the door. You couldn't understand a word; all you could see was the footboard of Delia's bed, a modern chrome thing; and it was very cold in the hallway.

After that, when you awoke too early and found yourself alone, you went out to the barn to smoke cigarettes, long ones. You were careful to extinguish them. You sat upon a burlap sack filled with loam, next to the lawnmower, one that still functioned. It would be very bright outside when you awoke again, and there would be flecks of loam in your hair, and field mice would scatter as you wriggled your toes inside his Turkish socks.

When you did ask Victor to identify that unknown Slavic language, he replied in gutteral polysyllables. It made you quiver with excitement. He still spoke French in bed, to you alone.

It was important for you to realize that Delia felt no guilt about sleeping with your husband. You would not have allowed her to. Guilt was your perogative, just as leave-taking was hers. You could have been happy with a menage à trois. (You already had a menage à trois, was one way to look at it.) But when Delia woke you up on foggy mornings, weeping onto your flannel nightgown, then you had misgivings. Why should she complain of his fondness for limericks, his sweet-tooth, the quadraphonic sound? Weren't they his perogative? But Delia wasn't convinced. She claimed to find his imagination ordinary.

One day she intruded into your deep sleep, first with a tentative clutching and reclutching of the doorknob, then with a brisk entrance. She admired the view from your window, made pleasantries.

"It's not what you think at all, Stace. We do it missionary position. And then in the morning he tells me he's dreamt of Natural History! All my dreams are symbolic—of that I'm sure. But I seem to have lost the capacity to be interested. I seem to be bored. Remember all the fun things we learned about the sex lives of the Melanesians?"

You nodded sympathetically. Of course, she was thinking of someone else, perhaps herself alone. You never studied anthropology together.

"The thing is, Stace, he's your husband. So it's not strange that I expect you to solve this dilemma." By then, Delia had spread herself around the armchair like a fur coat.

"You're right about that, he is my husband. And he's not boring. But I don't know how to make it more fun for you."

Delia was breathing heavily. She was tuning up her throat as if it were an instrument. "Oh Stace! What I could do with a little imagination!"

You knew something else: you could have continued sleeping, finished dreaming. In your dream, three or four raccoons and opossums were sitting down to dinner, and a middle-aged man was insisting that one of them say grace. Along with the animals, you resisted that suggestion by holding your silverware upright and pounding it on the wooden table, which began to split, slowly and distinctly. With a long pointer, the man kept progress with the pace of the split, and when a third of the table fell away, he said, "There goes California. No more avocados for you, my dear." It was your response to this remark that Delia's entrance had cut off.

So you responded to her, "You have imagination, Delia. I'll vouch for it. You just don't recognize it."

"I'd recognize it if it walked in right now, wearing socks. I'm not blind, you know."

"I think I'll go back to sleep."

Together in the bedroom, while listening with your inner ear to raindrops bouncing off the eaves, you discussed with Victor your plan to become pregnant. You mentioned reasons such as your age, financial security, your overactive ovaries, and your desire to know the pleasures of breast-feeding. Clearly, they were not the only reasons. Victor was able to discuss the issue while ignoring the assumption that he would be the father. He had a way of referring to "your" child that didn't bother you at all. He brought up the question of your fitness for maternity, as if it were a question of going into spring training.

"I'd be a good mother. I have the hands of a surgeon, the nesting instinct of an egret, the voice of Jenny Lind."

Victor regarded his perfect features in the mirror you had recently broken. His reflection refracted into a Cubist representation. You were lying on the bed, propped up by pillows. You were tempted to masturbate so that Victor could watch you in the mirror (if he stood at the correct angle). But since you had never masturbated before, you kept your hands pinned beneath the small of your back.

"Your wit, however, would be lost on your child until it reached the Age of Reason, assuming it survived the bombardment."

"I think you're being cruel. I'd understand a child. We could be related in so many ways."

"You can't even relate to your sister. And you're twins. Sprung from the same womb. Peas in a pod. With your child there'd be one inside, and you outside. You would feel the kicking and not recognize the impulse that motivated it."

"That's where a man can't understand motherhood. I'd be both inside and outside." Your hands leapt up from their nesting place and outlined a pregnant belly in the air above your flat abdomen. "Besides, Delia and I relate like the right and left hand."

"Talk on," he said. "I'm unconvinceable."

"You're so sure. Remember, you can always count on me."

Then there was the night you didn't use your diaphragm and didn't tell your husband. Afterward, you dreamt the same dream as always, of you and Delia becoming irrevocably confused: neither of you can swear to who she is; there are long corridors with birch trees growing inside; you and Delia holler at each other across the short white space, and the sound disappears into air—thus is all hope, of figuring out who is who, lost.

Certainly you were too self-conscious during the act. You wanted a child too much, and you didn't trust your own reasons. While you were kinetically aware of the slapping noise of bare bellies, of the tingling sensation produced by your heels pressed to the back of Victor's neck, you were thinking: Are we really making a baby now? Will I remember this all her life? Is there such a thing as the sixth sense? As woman's intuition? As the maternal instinct? Victor came with the same happy howl as always, then sank into the chilly outer regions of the bed. The temptation was to go to sleep at once, so that later it would all be a dream. But you shook him and raised yourself up on an elbow to stare into the shallows of his black-and-brown eyes. In them, of course, was you reflected. What did Victor have to say? "Go to sleep, my fat elf. You'll need that energy later." Only then, the dream.

In the days that followed, weatherless days, there was no way you could tell if Victor knew. You lay awake more often in order to sigh with relief. Where was Victor? What were the chances that he had reverted to an ancient taboo? Delia was the one with all that stored knowledge.

Victor wandered at random in the hallway and ended up in Delia's room. You could hear her pretending to be asleep, then awoken, then surprised. She had always had an expressive voice. Out in the barn you smoked cigarettes. At first, you were afraid to touch the cold metal of the lawnmower's handle; then your hand encircled it, and warmed it. An eerie blue light filled the garden that morning. The ducks quacked and quacked as if they thought the sky had made a mistake.

Other mornings you heard whisperings in Delia's room that could not even drive you away. You threw pillows at the heating vents. But her chrome bed had ceased to noisily rub scars into the wall; her moans were imitations of their former selves. She was as morbid as ever, but her imagination no longer functioned. The misery she complained of, in whispers, was old material. Her responses to questions could not be described as answers.

The rubber soles of your boots compressed against the pavement. Cars honked; their squawking was like the ducks'. There was a large, uneven building. The top was as rectangular as ever, but the bottom ten floors seemed to ooze out, like mud caught in the shifting terrain. The wind pressed your skirt against your thighs, where it stayed as if glued. You tugged at it.

George Sleaves' office was on the top floor. Once, your father's office was next door, and you dragged sticky fingertips across the tinted glass. This time, looking out and down upon the financial district and the harbor, you tried to induce a state of vertigo in yourself. Your head refused to spin. You were wearing a black skirt and a black turtleneck sweater drawn tight at the waist by a satin belt with a rhinestone buckle, and yellow rubber boots. The big question had been about the boots: whether to go with your own, or borrow Delia's red ones with the tassels at the backs.

George's grey flannel suit did not look frayed at the edges. What made you think it might? He said, from behind his hand-hewn desk, "Quite a view, eh Stacey? And you look picturesque beside it. You should come in more often. There's always something to discuss, an amendment here, a codicil there."

You sat down and placed your elbows on the desk and your jaw in your palms as if your head weighed a ton. Your chin jutted out over the blotter. "My father used to say the view distracted him."

"Your father was a remarkable man."

"Yes. And you know, we've had a strange time being orphans. Stranded into our adulthood. It doesn't seem like much, I know, but we find it quite intense. At first I planned to seek out an older, wiser man, to replace my father. Yet I married someone our own age. Mine and Delia's. Delia says she'll never marry. I suppose there are a lot of things she'll never do."

George turned the typed documents on his desk face down. "How is Delia?"

"Oh, she's fine." You couldn't tell whether or not this interlude was meant to deflect your intentions.

George turned the documents back over. You thought that you were actually reading the upside-down words, but it was just the aesthetic experience of admiring runic script.

"Is there something for me to sign?"

Of course there was, and it was one of your small pleasures to sign your name along lines already marked with pencilled initials. It happened so quickly. These papers were mere formalities, meant to insure a smooth transfer of capital from your trust fund to a trust fund to be automatically established at the birth of a child. George preferred to deal with, and include, all possibilities. His gold pen still between your fingers, George placed his large hand atop yours. You could count the dark hairs that dotted the back of it. The hair on his head was bushy, but he did not seem an otherwise hirsute man. He said in a low voice, "May I?" and then kissed you. You responded with a certain demureness. You had a momentary flash of fear that he knew your every thought; that he would take you along so far and then expose your lust to the world. What world? Who cares? You regained your composure. When he kissed you again, your tongue darted in and out of his mouth, like a tropical fish. When you both stopped for breath, you noticed his perfect white teeth for the first time. You were immensely pleased, as if they affirmed the correctness of what you were doing. You continued kissing, and traded anecdotes about your father's eccentricity and his daughter's adventures until noontime, when his secretary left the outer office and both doors could be locked.

You were surprised by the tan George had managed to maintain well past the sunny months. Naked, he filled the room. His uncontrolled hair seemed to graze the ceiling. He stacked his unfolded clothes upon the desk, his underwear forming the pinnacle. You arranged yours in a pile next to his. Besides the snow-white underwear, the colors were predominantly black and grey. You wished you had a wide-angle lens to take a photograph of the desk and the clothes and the city's skyscrapers in the background. Making love on the couch you kept your eyes open and focused on the picture window. Two possibilities occurred to you. One was that a window-washer would swing into your range of vision, and that after a few moments of not noticing the energetic lovers he would begin to pound on the window and demand to be let in. The windows were, of course, hermetically sealed. The other was that a misdirected sea gull would fly into its reflection in your window, that its skull would shatter, and that it would fall thirty-five stories to the sidewalk below. You would not see, but only imagine, the commotion, or lack of, its drop from the sky would cause among the passers-by. In fact, the picture window began to fog up. George reached down, and holding your legs by the knees, folded them, one at a time, around his shoulders. Your own acquiescence excited you. (And frightened you. The tiny embryo was surely being impaled against the farthest wall of your womb.) When you shed stray tears as you recited your litany of pleasure, it was also because of the pain. George seemed to resist an impulse to press his cupped hand against your mouth. Your own impulses were, by then, happily drained away. And soon, he was dozing atop of you. You could hardly breathe. The picture window had lost its interest.

Getting dressed was amusing. You made comments about each other's clothes that were funny at the time. He mentioned other documents that might need signing, but you refrained from making appointments. You were anxious to have your lunch of avocados and cream cheese on date-nut bread.

George said, "You're actually hungry?"

"Of course."

Was it merely a desire for privacy—the intimacy between the eater and the eaten—that kept you from offering him some of your lunch? Movements could be heard in the outer office. George kissed your cheek. You pressed your palm to his groin. He held your neck between his thumb and forefinger. You separated from each other like the egg from the yolk.

Victor's hands were red from the auroral cold and bore the imprint of the axe's handle. He had been laying in a supply of wood for the even colder months. You were wide awake, but still in your flannel nightgown. The white of the kitchen was somewhat diffused.

He said, "Did you know that ursa is the most recently evolved of all carnivores?"

"You mean, a bear?"

"Of course. Ursa walks with his soles on the ground, in plantigrade fashion, like man. Each foot has five digits, ending in nonretractile claws."

You held your hands up, palm forward, to the early light.

"But," said Victor, "the cycles their lives revolve around are not psychological, they are dietary. Usually gaining weight beforehand, ursa sleeps fitfully through the winter, but this does not constitute true hibernation."

You asked, "Is that what we're going to do?"

Were you surprised to find yourself out in the night just as Delia was overturning the canoe in the middle of the pond? It certainly is true that coincidence played no part in your life. The ducks maintained the enraptured silence of a good audience. Delia kept herself underwater, and beneath the cavity of the canoe, with straight and unrelenting arms; her hands clutched the gunwales. There was no way you could actually see that (her body, her arms), but it was as clear as if the spotlight and underwater cameras were focused on her. You stripped to a reflective white in the moonlight and swam through the algal water to her rescue. Delia was unconscious and bloated. After righting the canoe you tried to push or pull her aboard, but the dead weight was too much. So you secured her head in the crook of your arm and towed her ashore. She began sputtering complaints against this rough treatment as you approached the willow branches that overhung the pond and clotted the water. Back in the house, she handed you her note. You had both hung your clothes over the firescreen and were seated, naked, in front of the fire. Your bodies mirrored each other, gave no hint of who had been underwater the longest. Victor could be heard splitting kindling behind the house.

It read: "Stacey. After so much nothing I seem to have come up with a reason for these activities of mine. I *do* mind it all: the orphanhood, our spooky resemblance, our perverse domesticity, my inability to attach myself, my dreams of animals, *your* dreams of animals. It is as if I am a coffin for a family of gnomes who are clawing at my stomach lining to be released. Does this sound like the other ones? My distress is real. Without me, yours will probably be also."

You were grateful that Delia had left her chair and the room before you had to look up from the page. A certain sadness occurred to you, with the same novelty of discovering one's own sexuality. The sound of axe against wood had stopped. To be heard now were Delia's overgrown toenails clacking against the tiles of the bathroom floor.

In the grocery store, you overheard this bit of conversation: "My dear, I have fallen arches, weak ankles, small toes, and a cracked tarsal, always have. So the higher I get off the ground . . ." In the frozen food aisle you passed the speaker, a woman, and looked down anticipating platform shoes. Nothing of the sort. The face of the woman beside you in the dairy section was marked by a purple blotch in the shape of a heart. That moved you. She had both cats and dogs; you assumed plural from the way her cart was laden. She liked ice cream. Perhaps she found it numbing. You, too, found it to be cold. You gazed in horror at the green and orange vegetables in your own cart. The discovery that the bag-boy wore make-up cheered you. The pale blue eye-shadow could have been painted on his lids by Bonnard, the touch was so sure, so understated. Chris smiled at you through stained teeth. He always carried your bags to the car. Had you been blind to his eyelids before?

In the parking lot he said, "Nice day for polar bears, huh, Mrs. D.?"

Assenting, "And for ducks, and for you and me."

"Not for me anymore, Mrs. D. They've blown my cover for good this time. They're sending me back to school. They found out my age."

You nodded as if this history were familiar to you. It was not. Chris has always looked like an undernourished adult to you.

"Well, it's been nice knowing you, Mrs. D. I'll probably be back in a year or two, but you can never tell what may be just around the corner."

If there was one thing you were sure of, it was that you were not the twin who suffered from car sickness. Yet halfway home you pulled the car onto the sidewalk and vomited into the culvert. The nausea did not pass.

In the intervening weeks, you became preoccupied with your physical body. The veins in your hands and forearms seemed more pronounced. The sensation of your head puffing up, and then deflating, was disturbing at first. Then it became one of the landmarks along which your days were plotted. Nausea stayed with you, a passenger. You did not like to be located far from a bathroom. You watched yourself urinate, began to notice distinctions in color. When the house was full of shadows, you even noticed differences between the way Delia looked and the way you imagined yourself. It was eerie when the handsome doctor told you that you were pregnant, as if you hadn't known. (He seemed pleased. He assured you that he still made house calls.) One hand cupping a breast, wanting to catch the exact moment of swelling, the other flat against your abdomen, was the way you walked around. Your domestic activities narrowed down to fixing yourself sweet and sour foods in the afternoon, bitter and delicious.

A pertinent question was: whom to tell first, Delia or Victor?

You poked your head out the bedroom door because you had heard his muted footfalls. Victor was heading for the bathroom in his viyella robe and Turkish socks. He looked at you expectantly. An expression that was almost tender spread across his face. You spoke, "Guess who's pregnant?" And then stepped back and shut the door. Through the barrier you could hear him breathing in the hallway, deciding on the exact phrasing of his response to what was surely a Socratic question.

"I give up. Who?" He winced as he said it.

"I am. That's who."

"Mine, I suppose?"

"Who else's?" This question stayed unanswered, like a fruit in a deserted orchard that will never be plucked.

"You must be pleased."

"I am. I feel fulfilled. Say you're pleased too. Say so." That tone of pleading was not supposed to enter your voice, with its diminished volume. "Say you want it." You were supposed to be so complete within yourself that it would be an effort to recognize the dim figures that inhabited the house with you.

Victor pushed the door open, and you stepped back to let it swing fully. Then he hugged you. It occurred to you that he wanted to feel the new presence in your belly, wanted to develop a rapport with it that was all his own. He wouldn't speak, but made love to you, back to front, of course.

One morning, you found this note suspended from your doorknob by a piece of string. "Dear Stacey. I am absolutely sure of this one. I shot myself in the barn last night. I suppose if you had known of the existence of a gun we could have continued this serial indefinitely. But I had to have this one way out, and I had to finally dissolve all the flimsy excuses. You will know that this is the final one because I am going to tell you how I love you, as a half, as a reflection, as an echo, even as yourself—for as much as we have been able to make the distinction between one and the other. So: of course I know that you are pregnant. And not just because you vomit every morning, so regularly, so self-satisfied. I have to believe that the preparation I've given you is worth something, and that you will therefore be calm enough not to miscarry. I wake up at night with a thrashing in my belly. Surely, something wants to get out."

And you ran out to the barn in Victor's Turkish socks. Delia looked comfortably asleep beside the lawnmower. Pale crushed cigarette butts littered the wooden floor. Her right hand rested atop the gun with the same folded grace of draperies in late Renaissance paintings. The side of her head which lay tilted against the sack of loam was blown away. For a second, you regarded thoughtfully the exposed flesh covered with clotted blood. Then you shrieked, for the space of minutes or hours. The flapping of the wings of ducks fleeing their pond could be heard overhead. You closed your eyes, and when you opened them you were still watching Delia's absolute stillness. But from a different vantage point—because you were seated beside her, holding her other hand, stroking her belly, reassuring her.

It was lucky that Victor had chopped so much wood earlier, because that exercise no longer interested him. He let you wear his socks all the time now, and you hardly ever went out, you were so big and sleepy.

He did tell you one more thing: "The issue of the family Marsupialia, born in such a vulnerable embryonic condition, make their way to the warmth and nourishment of the pouch. Those fortunate enough to survive this arduous journey may succeed in attaching themselves to their mother's nipples, which then swell and become firmly fastened—almost physically fused—to the mouth tissues of the babies. Although marsupials are not entirely silent, none, none utter grunts of contentment or even cries of hunger when young."

You drink tangerine juice from a mug engraved with Delia's name. Tangerines come from another climate. You catch yourself thinking: Another era. But don't eras indicate dynasties, prevailing economic attitudes, artistic restatements, shifting in the geodetic table? Your juice came from the white refrigerator. It needs defrosting. When you put your head inside, it reacts analytically to the cold air. That is, it can feel each cell of itself separating and fleeing into the vacuum. And it is true, that every cell of your skull, cranium, hair, and epidermis is a separate entity, as individual and ineluctably connected as Delia and you.

FAUST AND HIS WORLD OF PLASTIC

DAWSON JACKSON

1
I looked out of the window
And saw a world of

Plastic—plastic and people,
Nothing else.

Is that
What we want? To

Reshape the earth—from a thing that's
There, in its own right, as we are,

To a blank extension
Of ourselves? An artificial

Universe, recreated by
Us? Us! Which is, no

Universe: a universe that's
Just us. And an us who

Wish to do
This thing.

Conquest! discovery! transformation, change,
The new! . . . How

Can cripples gain
Such power?

Who
But cripples want to?

•

The world which we are given
Is one of
Beings, creatures: who fight, and
Love, us back—give us, thus,

Reality, fulfilment, and
Keep us in our place.

The world which we are
Trying to make is one
Without resistance, that cannot
Fight back—in which
Is only

Us, and our needs'
Surface
Satisfaction: without other

Beings
In it—without reality—and
Between which and us
Cannot (since there are
No other beings
In it) be
Love. That

Is what I mean by plastic.

•

Succeeding, we'll destroy the
World we're given: till
Its destruction
Destroys
Us. A plague of

Mice, eventually, is
Wiped out
By diseases—or destroys
The food it has to live on: and

The balance rights itself.

We may destroy
The earth, the solar system,
This galaxy, all the
Stars we know. Then—
The burnt patch, where we were,
Grows over. Such is

The stupendous
Size of things, beyond our sight, that
Whatever we
May do is
Small. We need not fear

That we may destroy
God. We are not
Milton's Satan.

Yet what we
Are doing
Matters. Matters very much:
For us.

2
What does
Faust

Want? His
Each desire 's
Satisfaction; as it
Assails him.

Like a baby.

What he really
Wants—he does not
Know: has no
Name
For. So
He cannot ask it of the devil.

If he'd asked
Love—he'd have
Got it:
From another quarter.

Faust damns
Himself. Crippled—he
Does not know what to want.

·

Motorcars: there's
Magic, for you!

And what have we got?
All those

People shut up in their little
Locomotive cells—jammed
In the towns, and rushing through the
Disappearing country, in

Environment-destroying lethal
Bits of tin.

What did we
Want? To enrich
Our life with
Nature, our life with
One another? No.
Power:

Speed; escape from
Reality, from the flesh; ego's
Omnipotence: restraintless
Flying through the air.

And
Our Helen
Vanishes.
Nor her, nor necromancy,

We need—but a
Loved
World: loved
Like a wife.

•

If you know what is
Worth wanting, you

Have it, already.

3
Power. Or
Love. Take your choice.

Rape her: or, loving,
Give pleasure.

Conquering, you
Flatten out the earth—

And meet nothing, on it,
But yourself.

Loving, you let things be
In their variety: and

Live—enlarged by
Their life—in them.

Prison, one way. The other—
Liberation.

FEELINGS ON GROWING OLD

GREGORY CORSO

When I was young I knew only one Pope
            one President
            one Emperor of Japan
When I was young nobody ever grew old
            or died
The movie I saw when I was ten
            is an old movie now
            and all its stars
            are stars no more
Now it's happening . . . As I age
the celebrated unchanging faces of yesterday
            are aging drasticly
Popes and Presidents die without aging
            Rock stars too
So suddenly have matinee idols grown old!
            and those starlets
            now grandmothering starlets!
And as long as I live
            movie stars keep on dying—

What's to be done?
Stop reading newspapers?

Die myself?
Would that make Popes and Presidents deathless?
Movie stars ageless as their celluloid selves?
Yes, when I was young
        the old always seemed old
        as if they were born that way
And the likes of Clark Gable, Vivien Leigh
        seemed forever
Yes, now that I am older
        the old of my youth are dead
        and the young of my youth are old
Wasn't long ago
        in the company of peers
        poets and convicts
        I was the youngest for years
I entered prison the youngest and left the youngest
Of Ginsberg Burroughs & Kerouac . . . the youngest
And I was young when I began to be the oldest
At Harvard a 24 year old amongst 20 year olds

Alive Kerouac was older than me
But now
        I'm a year older than him
And 15 years older than Christ
Ye gods! in the Catholic sense
        I am 15 years older than God!
        and getting older!

Women . . . the women of my youth
        shades of Villon!
To think that once I wanted to give
        undying love to the beauty & form
        of a lady of 40 in 1950
I beheld her recently she in her 70's
        in a long black dress
        her once magnificent ass
        all sunken flat!
How cruel the ephemera of fleshéd proportion
Poor Marilyn Monroe!

No Venus she,
> the mortal goddess of beauty & love
> was but a hairy bag of water
—and so are we all
At least stone goddesses with all their amputations
> maintain the beauty of their ruin

Strange too:
When I was 20 my father was 40
and he looked & behaved like he did
> when I was 5 and he 25
and now that in 2 years I'll be 50
> a half century old!
> and he 70
it's me not him
> always getting & looking older
Yes, the old, if they live, remain old
but the young the young never remain
. . . they're the stuff what becomes old

No, I don't know what it's like being old . . . yet
I've a grilfriend in her early 20's
I don't feel like a dirty old man!
And I've a son just 2 and a half
In 20 years I'll be 70
She'll be in her early 40's
> and he in his early 20's
> and it'll be the year 2000!
And everybody will celebrate
and drink and love and have fun
while me poor me
> will be pruny and even more toothless
> and bony-assed
> and ineivtably stained with pee
. . . and yet, yet shall planes crash
And Popes, matinee idols, yet shall they die

And somehow
> somehow with all this oldingness

I see with a loving smile
        Life
        a hundred years from now
        like a hundred years ago
with all the comings came
and all the goings gone

TRIBUTES TO LOUIS ZUKOFSKY

(1904–1978)

Edited by Hugh Kenner, Celia Zukofsky, and David Gordon

TABLE OF CONTENTS

Basil Bunting 149

George Oppen 150

Ronald Johnson 150

Robert Creeley 151

Hugh Kenner 154

Hayden Carruth 158

Guy Davenport 159

Louis Zukofsky 164

Hugh Kenner 166

Charles Tomlinson 175

David Gordon 178

POUND AND "ZUK"

Basil Bunting

Pound's conversation was as full as his writings of genial maxims about making poetry, with the advantage that you could sometimes ask him to exemplify. His maxims were by no means always compatible with one another and still less with his own practice, yet they were never negligible. You thought about them—at any rate I did—and might profit from them.

Zukofsky, about 1929 or '30, had selected a few of Pound's more cogent maxims and rephrased them (alas! in what I took to be the obscure dialect of pedants), and he lived up to them and seemed to apply them to all he wrote in verse.

Pound made a few verbal strictures on my early poems, and he also did for my "Villon," at lightning speed, much what he had done far more momentously for Eliot's *The Waste Land;* he struck out much, amended a little, and told me to amend more. Later he retrieved some discards of mine from my wastepaper basket and insisted on having them published. I am not sure whether I am pleased about that.

Zukofsky however went through poems I sent him very meticulously, word by word, making suggestions here, fierce strictures there, and sometimes recommending the wastepaper basket. (He would also sometimes express enthusiasm for particular lines or passages.) This he did when, as in the early '30s, I think his admiration for my work was very tepid indeed; and he kept it up later, after he had changed his mind. Even after the war he helped greatly with "The Spoils" and still took pains, though less lavishly, with the manuscript of "Briggflatts."

A systematic man might possibly have derived all Zukofsky's critical help from Pound's *obiter dicta,* but I am even less systematic than Pound, so that Zukofsky's patience and severity were very valuable to me . . . as they were to Carlos Williams—so WCW told me long ago.

It took more than two thousand years of violent opposition to make the Jews as stubborn as many of the best of them are. Sometimes I don't like it; but everyone admires and even loves that stubbornness in Spinoza, Zukofsky's favourite amongst philosophers;

and the stubbornness L.Z. used in his verse and in his detailed criticism is just as admirable.

Pound was volatile, malleable and acute. Zukofsky was relatively unchanging, if somewhat slower to perceive.

MY DEBT TO HIM

George Oppen

Zukofsky's brilliance—his example and his brilliant comment—were revelatory to me—my first step beyond adolescent poetry—and I thank you for this opportunity to remember again my debt to him.

from "WOR(1)DS 45, A SPIRE FOR THE DEATH OF L. Z."

Ronald Johnson

this is
happening
on the surface of a bubble
time and again
fire sculpt of notwithstanding
dark
the whole portal world
in choir
when the wind's bright horses
hooves break earth in thunder
that,
that is paradise
Lord Hades, whom we all will meet
crackling up
like a wall of prairie fire

in sommersault silver
to climb blank air
around us
to say then head wedded nail and hammer to the
work of vision
of the word
at hand
that is paradise
this is called spine of white cypress
roughly cylindrical
based
on the principle
of the intervals between cuckoos
in Mahler's First, Delius'
On Hearing
these are the carpets of
protoplast, this
the hall of crystcycling waltz
down carbon atom
this, red clay
grassland
where the cloud steeds clatter out wide stars
this is

For L.Z.

Robert Creeley

It is an *honor* to know men and women of genius and probity, because we live, finally, in a human world, and however we would dispose ourselves toward that world otherwise the case, it is the human one which makes the most intimate and significant judgment. For myself and others of my generation, our elders in the art were extraordinary example and resource. Despite a chaos of restrictive generalization, we had nonetheless the active, persistent functioning of example: Ezra Pound, William Carlos Williams, Basil Bunting, Louis Zukofsky—to note those most dear to my own heart.

My first information of Zukofsky was in the dedications of two books crucial to my senses of poetry, Ezra Pound's *Guide to Kulchur* ("To Louis Zukofsky and Basil Bunting strugglers in the desert") and Williams' *The Wedge* ("To L.Z."). It was, however, Edward Dahlberg who gave me my first active sense of Zukofsky's situation and urged me to invite him to contribute to *The Black Mountain Review,* which happily I did, resulting in the publication of a section from "A"-12 (BMR #5) and "Songs of Degrees" and "Bottom: On Shakespeare, Part Two" (BMR #6). In the meantime Robert Duncan had arrived in Mallorca and become a close friend and mentor, and it was he who showed me Williams' review of *Anew* as well as texts of Zukofsky himself. Then, in 1955 as I recall, while teaching at Black Mountain and visiting briefly in New York, I determined to meet Zukofsky if possible, and so one evening attempted the subway out to Brooklyn with just twenty cents in my pocket. As luck would have it, I overshot my destination, spent my remaining dime on correcting my error, and finally arrived tentative, confused, and literally penniless.

It's to the point, I believe, that such acts be remembered, especially when they define the possibilities of human responsibility and choice. As I came into the house on Willow Street, to be met by these extraordinarily dear and tender people, I somehow determined it would be best for all concerned if I revealed my predicament immediately, and I tried to. But Louis asked a favor of me, as he put it, saying that Celia was altering an overcoat for him, and it would help the sense of fitting required if I would put it on so that he might see how it looked. I did, and immediately Louis said, "There, it's yours!" Or words to that effect, because I cannot remember clearly what literally he did say, being then so distracted by the generosity of the gift and the fact that I had still to tell them I was broke. Finally I got *that* said, and their response was the specific coin required for the subway, *and* a five-dollar bill to go with it, *and* a substantial lunch for the trip back to Black Mountain next day.

And it never changed. Always that shy, intensive warmth, that dear, particular care. In fact, the last time I saw them together was in New York—we had met the day previous, by blessed accident, in the street—and I had come up to see them where they were now living in a residential hotel off Central Park. Again, as luck would have it, there was a torrential thunderstorm through which I walked a considerable distance, and arrived, dripping and wet to the skin. My coat was taken from me and hung up over the bathtub to dry. I was sat down and given hot coffee to warm me up, etc., etc. When Celia asked me if I'd like cream, I said, yes, if it were simple—which it proved not to be. So she gave me a spoonful of vanilla ice cream, to act as cream for the coffee, and then a full dish of it, in the event I might enjoy it for its own sake. And *then* we talked.

If I try to isolate my senses of Louis Zukofsky from those memories now, I neither can nor can I see the reason to. He taught me so much, in so many ways. Without the least trying, so to speak, the measures of person, of conduct, of art, which he constituted, are all of a factual piece. Again I think of that frail man's walking me late at night to the subway entrance, so I wouldn't have difficulty finding it, despite the effort it must have been for him to confront those streets at that hour, and his walk back alone. I remember "raise grief to music"—"the joy that comes from knowing things"—"the more so all have it"—"upper limit music, lower limit speech"—"love lights light in like eyes"—"he got around. . . ." And if I misquote, then I do—because this is the practical, *daily* company of Louis Zukofsky for me, the measure of his father, "everybody loved Reb Pincos because he loved everybody. Simple. . . ."

Thankfully, I was able at times to make clear my respect—in various reviews and notes, in the rather crunky introduction to "A" 1–12 (New York: Doubleday, 1967) with its several misprints, etc. And, more privately, I could argue the case at times, as Hugh Kenner will remember, apropos "The Winds / agitating / the / waters." Which certainly *looked* easy, as he said, but trying, did discover was otherwise—and then wrote the primary review of "A" 1–12 (in its first Origin edition), in which he rightly qualifies the *art* of Zukofsky's practice as so much the more accomplished than Auden's, whose *Homage to Clio* he was also reviewing. Etc. These "arguments" will die with us too. L.Z.—never.

LOUIS ZUKOFSKY: ALL THE WORDS

Hugh Kenner

"Eyes," he wrote, is pronounced "I's"; language blinks, his eye was unblinking:

Not the branches
half in shadow

but the length
of each branch

Half in shadow

As if it had snowed
on each upper half

Louis Zukofsky took pleasure in a language whose traffic signals—"not" and "but"—sound (Knott & Butt) like stand-up comedians; a language—he could remember learning it, didn't grow up with it—where detailing two ways for branches to be half in shadow entailed saying words, "length" and "each," that you pronounce like kin-words to "branch." Moreover "shadow" and "had snowed" seem trying to be anagrams: just one letter left over. He pared shavings away to leave such impacted curiosities noticeable.

Not crossword curiosities he thought, something profound here. Not anything people do, not even lovemaking, is more intimately physical than speech. Hence "something must have led the Greeks to say *hudor* and us to say *water*": Some remote mystery of the body that sways to music and is chilled by fright (and eats tiny cookies on airplanes).

Louis Zukofsky's own body—"pulled forward," someone said, "by the weight of his eyebrows"—seemed a weed to gauge verbal winds. Our dog Thomas, we used to suppose, could nudge him over without thinking, though in fact Thomas never did. It was Louis rather who altered Thomas forever, by grouping him with Thomas Aquinas as a manifest contemplative. Furrows of anxious thought have been evident on Thomas's brow ever since.

The tiny cookies—any number of them, as though in foresight of a skyjacking and a long siege—were baked and carefully wrapped in aluminum foil by Celia before the hazardous flight from Port Jefferson, N.Y., all the way to Baltimore. Celia was Louis' collaborator, his virtual alter ego. Even their handwriting looked alike, and the notebooks in which they worked out their strange "Catullus" resist casual decisions as to which hand (hers) wrote the Latin and the glosses, which (his) the endlessly punning equivalents—*Irascibly iterating my iambics* for *Irascere iterum meis iambis.* "I want to breathe," he said, "as Catullus did." Symbiosis could scarcely farther go, he with Celia, both with Catullus.

If one obligation of language was to breathe, another was to the road you scan with your eyes. And eye and music and lithe bodies meet in the woods where "Gentlemen cats / With paws like spats" prowl round in their nightly dance.

Ezra Pound's wife, Dorothy, could smile after forty years about the lines on the cats. A lifelong painter, she'd responded to the very young man who also lived through his eyes by drawing Egyptian cats on his typescript. That was in Rapallo in 1928; Pound had sent Zukofsky a check (never cashed) to help with the boat fare. There followed decades of mutual respect; in 1957 Zukofsky was reporting Pound's tolerant exasperation with the visitors he was getting by then, so unformed their conversation began and ended with "Grampa, haow do yew spell 'Kat'?"

By the time I met Louis in 1965 he'd become a virtuoso of hypochondria, the complaints generally starting with his feet, on which he'd tried every kind of shoe, yes, including Earth Shoe, with no amelioration. Just a few years earlier there'd still been, reportedly, "traces of a Fred Astaire charm and vertigo," something I saw just once, in a motel in Orono, Maine, where we all converged to help a university commemorate Pound.

He would dance, he suddenly announced. He smiled and limbered septuagenarian legs, forgetting that his feet were supposed to be hurting; dipped his shoulders, cocked his head. A straw skimmer would have completed the effect. But he'd talk a bit first; *then* he'd dance. . . . Now—but first some more talk; then shall I dance? It was like Danny Kaye in *The Inspector General,* with the difference that Kaye danced to keep from having to talk. In forty-five minutes of scintillating monologue Louis never did dance, but finally promised to another time.

The dance now seems as vivid as if it had happened, an effect familiar to readers of Zukofsky's verse, where brisk goings-on often seemed to caper just to one side of the words. A limber and dapper bachelor indeed of thirty-five it must have been who was courting Celia that long-ago year.

"Married (1939) Celia Thaew": What kind of name, I wondered, for heaven's sake, was Thaew? The kind of linguistic accident that made up the texture of Zukofsky's life. She should have been a Teyve (or Tevye, "as in *Fiddler on the Roof*"), but when her father came to Ellis Island the Immigration man had known just enough German to write T as *Th*, *ey* as *a umlaut*, *ve* as *w*, hence Thaew: much as Bernard Shaw spelled *fish* from enou*gh*, w*o*men, no*ti*on, hence *ghoti*. Except that the fish are proverbially speechless and the Teyves/Thaews were, as Homer would say, much-speaking.

As with Louis, who was born, he loved to assert, in the great East Side ghetto just about when Henry James was paying it a bemused visit (bemused: Muses). He grew up speaking Yiddish in a culture eager to provide. A man with the pen name Yehoash even imitated Japanese in Yiddish:

Rain blows, light, on quiet water
I watch the rings spread and travel
Shimaunu-San, Samurai,
When will you come home?—
Shimaunu-San, my clear star

—so runs Zukofsky's imitation of Yehoash. "Hiawatha," even, was available in Yiddish, and reading it was one of Zukofsky's spurs to learn English.

As he did; who better? Not I. Though my trade is professing "English," when the Zukofskys came to Baltimore I felt (anew) a gross ignorance of the language. They knew, to begin with, the name of simply everything, notably every sprig of vegetation, every flower. (Look this instant toward greenness; can you name the first thing you see?)

Beyond the name (and naturally the Linnaean binomial) they also knew, especially Louis knew, every remote shading the *Oxford English Dictionary* had recorded for 1,500 years' usage: likewise associated legends and private lore. And in "Eighty Flowers," which he'd meant for his eightieth birthday (1984) but luckily finished before his death this year [1978], you'll also have to remember that "flowers" can be a verb. That was one of his pleasures with English, anything could be any part of speech.

His chief books are *All*, the collected short poems which won't be wholly all till "Eighty Flowers" has joined them; *A*, the half century's magnum opus, which the University of California Press will be issuing in one volume late this year; *Prepositions*, his essays, another California agendum; and *Bottom: On Shakespeare*, the most idiosyncratic of homages to the greatest master of English. They will still be elucidating all of them in the twenty-second century, and perceiving what Zukofsky saw in words such as *a, the, from, to, about*.

He read "A"-11 for my microphone; on the tape a little dog (not Thomas) is audible two or three times. Louis rather welcomed the little dog's *obbligato*, something more even than he'd put into the poem. "A"-11 ("for Celia and Paul") causes the poem itself to console his wife and son after his death. He wrote it thirty-eight years ago, forethoughted. "Raise grief to music" is its burden. It reaches back seven centuries for its structure to the Cavalcanti canzone from which Eliot derived the opening of *Ash-Wednesday*, and forward into what was then the fore-time of Paul becoming a violin virtuoso, "the fingerboard pressed in my honor." Each stanza ends with "honor," and the last two are of dazzling intricacy. I'll let him speak the last lines:

> . . . four notes first too full for talk, leaf
> Lighting stem, stems bound to the branch that binds
>   the
> Tree, and then as from the same root we talk, leaf
> After leaf of your mind's music, page, walk leaf
> Over leaf of his thought, sounding
> His happiness: song sounding
> The grace that comes from knowing
> Things, her love our own showing
> Her love in all her honor.

DEAR LOUIS

Hayden Carruth

Forgive my taking so long. Illnesses have been troubling me, as, you say in your last, they have you. An existence without them? One hardly hopes. One works, and correspondence suffers, as we (friends) do too, and you're getting on with the new one, I'm sure. When you asked me to "guess" its title, after reading "A"-23, I said I couldn't but that for myself I'd choose "you Fourth out here," and you replied I was "welcome to it" but your own choice was "80 flowers." I should have known. As for your offer, I may take it, thanks to you and Callimachus. It says in epitome what I seem to have spent 20 years trying to say in extenso.

But "A"-24, what a wonder! *Celia's* masque, as you pointed out piquedly anent the poster (cubiculo). The five musicks. I've been "reading" them again, eye veering among the brilliants as if I were supine on a deck with a point of St. Elmo's fire at the masthead swinging among the stars. "If I concede to a metaphor," you wrote, "it must be good," and I felt a foolish moment. Not that I go with you to absolute exclusion, that being not the style of my "generation"; but indeed, indeed the technique is overworked and the "school," lo these hundred years, holding it, or any, to be intrinsically poetical . . . ! Off base.

So I envision you with your 80 flowers. Not easy, since in spite of all the letters we haven't met, the photos on your dust jackets being *no* help *at all!* Hazily at work, wreathed; doubtless in smoke, you being (I believe) addicted, like me, to tobacco, and, like me, doing a penance for it; penance so apparently out of proportion to the "sin." Work, work, work. For so little, all given away, as you say, in the hope of Ludwig W.'s one reader. You must be beyond what letter now—arbutus? lilac? The further condensation of *Bottom's* "alphabet of subjects," A to Z. Hard, God it must be hard. Good luck. Let me hear from you if you get the chance.

Love, ever,
Hayden.

SCRIPTA ZUKOFSKII ELOGIA

Guy Davenport

1

Eighteen songs set to music by his wife and fifty-three lines of type in six blocks of prose: this is Zukofsky's *Autobiography*, not his most eccentric work but certainly foremost as an eccentricity among the world's autobiographies.

1.1 The first of these songs is a buffoonery that Mr. Punch, Groucho Marx, Zero Mostel, and Buck Mulligan might sing in Elysium. It is a motet.

> General Martinet Gem
> Coughed Ahem, and Ahem, and Ahem
> Deploying the nerves of his men
> Right, and about face, to his phlegm.
> Their whangs marched up to the sky,
> His eyes telescoped into his head
> A pillow that as pillar of Europe
> He flung to his rupture Ahead.

1.2 The song is Zukofsky's world. Wrangle, Haig, Tojo, Goering.

1.3 The city in which Zukofsky lived he pictured by translating Catullus, as effective a recreation of the color, odor, and tone of its original as Orff's *Carmina Catulli* or Fellini's *Satyricon*.

1.4 The home in which Zukofsky lived is A. It contained two musicians, a poet, many books, and a television set.

2

"Has he published?" a professor asked at the committee meeting where I was trying to have a thousand dollars appropriated to bring Zukofsky to the University of Kentucky for a reading. But the same professor had probably never heard of Ausonius, Ts'ao Chih, or Stevie Smith.

2.1 How to answer the ignorant professor? The greatest of elegies for JFK ("A"-15

The fetlocks ankles of a ballerina
'Black Jack' Sardar with the black-
hilted sword black dangled in silver scabbard from
the saddle riderless rider
his life looked back
into silver stirrups and the
reversed boots in them.
. . .
John to John-John to Johnson)

2.2 The most original meditation on Shakespeare since Coleridge.

2.3 A translation of all of Catullus, all but unreadable except with great sympathy and curiosity, in which the English sounds like the Latin and is in the same meter. The beauty of this strange text is that it catches Catullus' goatish nasty with dignity, honesty, and a decent eye.

2.4 A.

2.5 Four volumes of lyrical poems, some of which rank among the finest of our century.

2.6 Some critical prose distinguished by its good sense and a pure style, some narrative prose distinguished by its whimsy, wit, and individual tone. LZ wrote prose as a race horse walks: nervous, skittery, itching for the bugle and the track.

3
His Shakespeare was a quattrocento Florentine.

4
Spinoza, Heraclitus, Wittgenstein, Bach, Jefferson, LZ: men with brotherly minds.

5
The engineering of his poetry, when revealed and demonstrated, will bring him close to Joyce.

6
He taught at a polytechnic institute, saw the Brooklyn Bridge daily

for thirty years, was fascinated by the shapes of the letter A (tetra-hedron, gable, strut) and Z (cantilever), and designed all his poetry with an engineer's love of structure, of solidities, of harmony.

7
Le Style Apollinaire. LZ is a scrupulous punctuator, with correcter parentheses, dashes, and semicolons than anyone else. Punctuation became dense as the railroad tracks went down, corresponding to their points, switches, signals, and semaphores. With the airplane, trackless and free, we get Apollinaire with no punctuation at all, Eliot, Pound, Cummings.

7.1 "A"-16 has no punctuation: it is airborne and speaks of the windflower. *80 Flowers* has no punctuation. But LZ's punctuation remains that of the city man for whom traffic signals are crucial. A-13 is a poem imitating a partita by Bach; "I"-75 is a four-lane highway.

8
The elegant engineering of *A* is an integral symbol.

9
The invention that distinguishes Zukofsky is the play of his wit. His instructors here were Shakespeare and the Baroque fiddle: a con-tinuum of sense that nevertheless interrupts itself all along the line to play, juggle quibbles, pun, dance in and out of nonsense, sustain cadenzas of awesome virtuosity, and switch the ridiculous and the sublime so fast that we are taught their happy interchangeability in a beautiful poised sensibility.

10
Jewish humor assumes a sweet intelligence. We feel the non-euclid-ean rightness of Sam Goldwyn's "Include me out" and "A man who goes to a psychiatrist ought to have his head examined." It was Freud who thought humor was the tension of anxiety released in a cryptogram that was sociable and congenial though threatening to the psyche as a decoded statement. As soon as we reach the anec-dote of the rabbi and the telephone in *A*, we know we are in good hands.

11

Zukofsky as a child thought that the uncircumcised couldn't urinate and was troubled to understand the radically different physiology of the *goyim*. Hence the concealed jokes about urine throughout *A*.

> Or as the Queen of British barmaids
> Before the Jury of her Pee-ers, Call
> Me Hebe, that means goddess of youth, Dears!
> ("A"-13)

Freudian blips zing across cockney fun: *Jewry* across *jury, hebe* (Hebrew) across *Hebe,* and in *Dears!* you can hear Fagin's lisp.

12

LZ was a prodigious and searching reader. He accepted books as his inheritance and spent a lifetime assaying the bequest.

13

He had the gift of the laconic. To Pound praising Mussolini in 1939, he said, "The voice, Ezra, the voice!" There must be hundreds of critical postcards like ones I've had from him. Of my Archilochos, "Something new!" Of *Flowers and Leaves*, "Yes, but where's the passion?" Of my Herakleitos, "Jes' crazy!"

14

Hearing that he frequently saw Djuna Barnes when he was out for a morning paper, I asked him if they exchanged pleasantries. "No," he said. "What do you say to The Minister's Black Veil?"

15

Fellow artists have treated him as a phenomenon, a force, a man (like Mallarmé or Whistler) to make obeisance to whether you understand his work or not. His appearance in Brakhage's *23rd Psalm Branch* is a characteristic of such homage. In a sequence about the Nazi concentration camps, Zukofsky's face is introduced as a motif. He was the kind of man who would have suffered Mandelstam's fate in Russia, Max Jacob's in France.

16

Joseph Cornell, Lorine Niedecker, Ronald Johnson, Charles Ives, Albert Pinkham Ryder, Emily Dickinson, Walt Whitman.

17

LZ was wise in the ways of a family as William Carlos in the ways of a community, Pound in the splendors of cultures. LZ was the most civilized of the three, an accomplished city dweller, a practical critic of place and history.

18

He would not talk on the phone if Celia were not there to hear the conversation.

19

Exploring the prehistoric caves at Les Eyzies in the Dordogne, he went into some that were too uncomfortable for Celia but described them so well that she felt she'd seen them.

20

A music of thought.

21

The precision of his mind demanded a heterogenous and improbable imagery. Surmounting difficulties was his *daimon*. When enough people became familiar with *A* so that it can be discussed, the first wonder will be how so many subjects got built into such unlikely patterns, and what a harmony they all make.

22

Two lives we lead: in the world and in our minds. Only a work of art can show us how we do it. The sciences concerned with the one aren't on speaking terms with those concerned with the other. Lenin once said that Socialism would inspire in the working man a love of natural beauty. One of my colleagues, a professor, once observed in front of my crackling, cozy fireplace that it was such a day as one might want to sit in front of a crackling, cozy fireplace if only people had such nice things anymore. I thought I was losing my mind: he really did not notice that he was sitting in front of a fire. His talk runs much to our need to expand our consciousness. LZ in his poetry is constantly knitting the two worlds together, fetching a detail from this one to match one in the other. And he saw into other minds with a lively clarity.

23
Spinoza with a body.

24
He propounded no theory, stood on no platform, marched in no ranks. He thought, he observed, he loved, he wrote.

25
Carmen 95 of Catullus is "to Ezra Pound." "Purvey me my intimate's core," it ends, "dear monument's all that there is, / let th' populace (tumid or gaudy) eat Antimacho." *Parva mei mihi sint cordi monumenta sodalis, / at populus tumido gaudeat Antimacho.*

A FOIN LASS BODDERS

Louis Zukofsky[*]

A foin lass bodders me I gotta tell her
Of a fact surely, so unrurly, often'
'r 't comes 'tcan't soften its proud neck's called love mm. . .
Even me brudders dead drunk in dare cellar
Feel it dough poorly 'n yrs. trurly rough 'n
His way ain't so tough 'n he can't speak from above mm. . .
'n' wid proper rational understandin'
Shtill standin' up on simple demonstration,
My inclination ain't all ways so hearty
Provin' its boith or the responsible parrty
Or what its vertus are to be commandin'
The landin' coincidin' with each gyration
Or if prostration makes it feel less tarty
Or 't' sumthin' to be seen by any smarty.

[*] Copyright © 1978 by Celia Zukofsky.

In that extenshun where memory's set up
Loove takes position, in condition right, till
It's light's diffusion from a penumbra
Of Mars' contention makes it stay het up
Wid such ignition, recognition, title,
The soul goes choosin' clothes, the heart longs sombre—
Once in that likeness it is cumprehended
Commended possible to the intellective
Faculties, subject ov place, and dhare abidin'
In such dimension whatev'r force betidin',
For so its quality has not descended
So splendid, perpetually effective,
Not so elective, but to thought subsidin'
Because othrewise it can't go presidin'.

No, it ain't vertue tho it is that comin'
Out as perfection, in connection righted
Not az benighted mind, you feel 't I tell you,
Beyond desert, you know it's justice—hummin'
Wid predilection worth correction blighted,
Somewut poor-sighted—its weakness, friends tell you—
Often it is such vertue 'ts death approaches
If 't poaches so its pow'rr plods and iz halted
In no wise vaulted but wid contr'ry weight you're
Surprised, not that it were opposite nature
Only a slight lack of perfection encroaches,
And such as no man can say 't's chance defaulted
Or that loove's bolted from its lordly stature
Worth the same, forgotten all nomenclature.

Living it ranges when its will is flaunted
Far beyond measure, from born treasure turnin',
Then not adornin' itself with rest ever
Moves so it changes color, laughs till 't weeps—haunted
Its image 's seizure 'n' fear, an' leisure yearnin',
Scarcely sojournin' in one place tho ever
You'll see that he was where worthy folk throve; the
New love, the quality 't has, moves to such sighing
So that descrying the thing's place man causes

Such clamour to rise, fired his passion pauses;
No one can know its likeness who don't prove the
Fact, love won't move tho it draws t' himself, aye 'n'
It don't go flying off to beds ov roses
Nor cerrtainly to pick large or small posies.

Like his own sweatheart's is love's disposition
So that his pleasure it seems has her assurance,
Breaking with durance to stand where he surges,
Not that the fleet darts of beauty lack vision,
Rather tried measure of fear is your pure ans-
wer to man's prurience when high spirit urges:—
And no one's able to know love by its features,
Complete ewers of whiteness aim to contain it,
Whose ears retain it the same don't see 'ts figure,
Coming from it man's led eye on love's trigger
Away from colour and apart from all creatures
Where sutures in darkness take the light, plane it,
Fraud can't sustain it, say faith is love's rigour
So that kindness comes forth but from his vigour.

You may go now assuredly, my ballad,
Where you please, you are indeed so embellished
That those who've relished you more than their salad
Days 'll hold you hallowed and away from shoddy—
You can't stand making friends with everybody.

LOOVE IN BROOKLYN

Hugh Kenner

Donna—"A foin lass"—*mi prega*—"bodders me": what proportion of
the great Canzone is literary convention? And what happens if its
substance be moved in the direction of *volgari eloquentia,* vernac-
ular speech? Speech of a time and place: Brooklyn: the 1930s.
Guido's *stil nuovo* was allegedly grounded on Florentine vernacular

of the 1290s, a diction of which we possess no tape recordings. Zukofsky's version of *c.* 1938 is a comic *tour de force* and a four-way commentary: on Guido's Canzone, on Pound's 1928 and 1934 versions, on the possibility of American local speech underpinning philosophic song. Literary historians are glib in their talk of speech. To make speech course through verse means imagining, impersonating a speaker.

Zukofsky's Brooklyn philosopher, having downed a few to loosen his tongue, rambles ingenuously through five long sentences before dismissing what he's uttered as a "ballad." He rhymes at every few words, the rhymes as if by accident mapping exactly the high craft of the *Donna mi prega,* where "Each strophe," Pound wrote, "is articulated by 14 terminal and 12 inner rhyme sounds, which means that 52 out of every 154 syllables are bound into pattern."

Pound saw little for English to do with the pattern save acknowledge it. Beyond offering an impression of sonoric intricacy in the first strophe of his 1928 version—

> I for the nonce to them that know it *call*
> having no hope at *all*
>   that man who is base in *heart*
> Can bear his *part* or wit
>   into the *light* of it,
> And save they know't *aright* from nature's *source*
> I have no will to prove Love's *course.* . .

—he made no effort to follow Guido's rules. Zukofsky did, to the letter: every rhyme in its place. Which is a way of saying that Zukofsky welcomed difficulties, the more arbitrary the better; but a way of saying, too, that he sensed a way to make this clotted discourse speakable. Read it in short phrases, with a rising inflection on every rhyme-word:

> 1a No, it ain't vertue
>   tho it is that comin'
> 2a Out as perfection,
>   in connection
>   righted

3a Not az benighted
                    mind, you feel 't I tell you,
1b Beyond desert, you
                    know it's justice—hummin'
2b Wid predilection
              worth correction
                    blighted,
3b Somewut poor-sighted
                    —its weakness, friends tell you—

Once you've dealt with your awe at the recognition of intricacy—
1a and 1b, 2a and 2b, 3a and 3b using identical sounds, with
internal rhyming in the 2s and a link-rhyme from 2 to mid-3—you
begin to realize how the rhyming cues a colloquial phrasing. This
speaker, jingling his key-chain, thinks in short takes, spinning out a
copiousness no one can stem. Sensing how talk and exactness tended
to diverge, Pound had avoided rhyming's claims because they inter-
fered with exact words: he sought, in a high literary exercise, the
impression of precision:

A lady asks me
            I speak in season
She seeks reason for an affect, wild often
That is so proud he hath Love for a name
Who denys it can hear the truth now . . .
                    (1934)

This version (from Canto XXVI) intends that "affect" shall carry
its technical aura, and screws up "reason" to a reasoner's pitch, and
throws emphasis on the monosyllables "wild" and "proud." The 1928
version [*Literary Essays*, pp. 155-57] had opened,

Because a lady asks me, I would tell
Of an affect that comes often and is fell
And is so overweening: Love by name.
E'en its deniers can now hear the truth. . .

—abandoned, we may guess, because the iambic base tended to
obligate "filler" words; "fell" depends on a rhyme, not on wildness

(the Italian is *fero*, from *ferox*) and a colon doesn't make Guido's explicit connection between Pride and the name of Love. To fashion something fit for the *Cantos* Pound revised away from this idiom, toward local accuracy, and without discarding the tang of the living voice he requires us to imagine some pretty special speech, "the conversation in the Cavalcanti-Uberti family," which he guesses was "more stimulating than that in Tuscan bourgeois and ecclesiastical circles of the period."

To posit a rarified speech wasn't L.Z.'s way. "A foin lass" is one by-product of his work on "A"-9, a *double* Canzone which in its first half fits to Guido's schema details culled from H. Stanley Allen's *Electrons and Waves: An Introduction to Atomic Physics* (Macmillan, 1932), from the '30s proletarian bible, Marx's *Capital* in the Everyman's Library translation (1932), and from the same author's *Value, Price and Profit* (an edition dated 1935). This enterprise may well have been prompted by a suggestion of Pound's, that Guido's tone of thought in 1290 perhaps seemed as subversive "as conversation about Tom Paine, Marx, Lenin and Bucharin would today in a Methodist bankers' board meeting in Memphis, Tenn." The voice throughout most of the first half of "A"-9 is that of a chorus of *things*, embodying a fancy of Marx's [*Capital*, Everyman edn., p. 58] that if artifacts could speak they would expound their disengagement from human use. Their diction is impacted, abstract, cumbrous:

Hands, heart, not value made us, and of any
Desired perfection the projection solely,
Lives worked us slowly to delight the senses,
Of their fire you shall find us, of the many
Acts of direction not defection—wholly
Dead labor, lowlier with time's offenses,
Assumed things of labor powers extorted
So thwarted we are together impeded—
The labor speeded while our worth decreases—
Naturally surplus value increases
Being incident to the pact exhorted:
Unsorted, indrawn, but things that time ceded
To life exceeded—not change, the mind pieces
The expanse of labor in us when it ceases.

This stanza, the third of the five-and-a-coda that consumed two years' work, 1938-40, afforded the following grid of rhymes:

```
. . . . . . . . . . . . . .value. . . . . . . . . . . . . .any
. . . . . .perfection. . . . . .projection solely
. . . . . . . . . . .slowly. . . . . . . . . .senses
. . . . . . . . . . . . .shall you. . . . . .many
. . . . . .direction. . . .defection wholly
. . . . . . . . . . . .lowly. . . . . . . .offenses
. . . . . . . . . . . . . . . . . . . . . . . .extorted
. . . . .thwarted. . . . . . . . . . .impeded
. . . . . .speeded. . . . . . . . . . . . .decreases
. . . . . . . . . . . . . . . . . . . . . . . . . .increases
. .sorted. . . . . . . . . . . . . . . . . .ceded
. . . . . .exceeded. . . . . . . . . . . . . .pieces
. . . . . . . . . . . . . . . . . . . . . . . . . . .ceases
```

Another two years' work a decade later (1948-50) fitted into the spaces between these rhymes a new set of terms from the *Ethics* of Spinoza (also Everyman edition); hence in the second half of "A"-9 we read,

Virtue flames value, merriment love—any
Compassed perfection a projection solely
Power, the lowly do not tune the senses;
More apt, more salutary body moves many
Minds whose direction makes defection wholly
Vague. This sole lee is love: from it offences
To self or others die, and the extorted
Word, thwarted dream with eyes open; impeded
Not by things seeded from which strength increases;
Remindful of its deaths as loves decreases;
Happy with the dandelion unsorted,
Well-sorted by imagination speeded
To it, exceeded night lasts, the sun pieces
Its necessary nature, error ceases.

We recognize not merely the same rhyming sounds, but in most cases the identical words, and are apt to find meaning in the few substitutions; thus it seems appropriate that in a new canzone that has changed the theme from "value" to "love" the words "increases" and "decreases" should have changed places, and the sweatshop foreman's "exhorted" have given way to "the dandelion unsorted." (Every stanza in the second half of "A"-9 encloses a flower, but nothing grows amid the machinery of the first half.)

Though 26 key words, and "52 out of 154 syllables" in each stanza are locked down by the pattern, it has proven possible despite these constraints to turn the stanza, the whole canzone, completely around. "It is like turning a horse in a stall completely around without leading it out of the stall: annihilated, reconstituted." (By analogous effort, the poem implies, it should be possible to turn human conditions around.)

Concurrent with an early stage of these labors, the "Foin lass" was virtually a *jeu d'esprit:* "a relief," Zukofsky said in a 1940 preface, and the fun he was having with it comes through the text. (Fun for this poet was like playing 4 chess games at once, as a relief from playing 20 at once.) He was also gaining practice in the difficult form, familiarizing himself with the sense of the Cavalcanti, and working himself free from what would have been intrinsic with Guido's Canzone as he received it, the idiom and rhetoric of Ezra Pound. Not that Pound is to be swept out of sight; in 1940 Zukofsky issued one of the rarest of twentieth-century bibliographic items, just 55 copies of a mimeographed packet of aids toward the comprehension of the first half of "A"-9, containing a gathering of Marx and Allen citations, a page of mathematical lore that doesn't concern us here, Guido's text, the two Pound versions, the "Foin lass," the "A"-9 stanzas, and a prose "restatement" of the latter. The intention, he said, was to have the 75 lines from "A"-9 "fluoresce as it were in the light of seven centuries of interrelated thought." Flourescence occurs when a substance of the proper composition is struck by invisible rays, so this metaphor tells us both that the atomic texture of "A"-9 is special, much there that doesn't meet the eye, and that what should concern us in the array of exhibits is not the bits and scraps "A"-9 picked up but the radiation of forces. (Pound had written of "magnetisms that take form, that are seen, or that border the visible," and again, "The mediaeval philosopher would probably have been unable to think the electric world, and *not* think of it as a world of forms.")

In this array the "Foin lass" is the strangest element save a fugi-
tive one stranger still: two stanzas of a yet slangier Brooklynese ver-
sion done by Zukofsky's friend Jerry Riesman. Stanza 2 of this runs:

It sets up 'n dat part memory hails from
An' pulls a quick change into a range of light
Very like at night when Mars' shadow comes down
An' remains. De heart gives it de flair to come
T'rough; d' soul—oomph. Its name's a feelin', same's "a sight
T'sore eyes." It's made: 'n' right den an' dere goes to town
After takin' shape from a form which is seen
In de bean only if ya foist get de drift;
In dat case it'll shift yet for a right guy'll stay
In place, dough it can't rest because it don't weigh
Down but spreads out like electric light, so clean
Is its sheen everywhere, 'cause it's got lift.
A swell gift; but 'tain't all fun, y' figger out de lay.
It can't show true color any udder way.

So we may compare for instance:

(1) In quella parte
        dove sta memoria
    Prende suo stato [Guido]
(2) In memory's locus taketh he his state [Pound, '28]
(3) Where memory liveth,
        it takes its state [Pound, '34]
(4) It sets up 'n dat part memory hails from [Riesman]

and finally,

(5) In that extenshun where memory's set up
    Loove takes position [Zukofsky]

—the latter already poised for the next rhyme:

                in condition right, till
It's light's diffusion from a penumbra
Of Mars' contention makes it stay het up
Wid such ignition, recognition, title. . .

Here it's suddenly an effort to stop quoting. Zukofsky has surpassed the amusingly idiomatic Riesman in one salient respect, that he keeps the sentence moving on, each phrase reaching forward for the next. This has entailed making the rhyme-words terminate phrases; Riesman put in all the rhymes too, but it's an effort to find them.

Zukofsky's colloquial games with meaning are subtler too. Thus Cavalcanti says that the shade on which luminous Love is formed comes from Mars and stays, *e fa dimora*. But for Zukofsky's streetwise guy it's Loove that stays, moreover stays het up, a meaning clamped firmly in place between a preceding rhyme, "set up," and a subsequent word, "ignition," a word Mr. Wise Guy would know, on his car-filled street. This speaker won't let us forget what he's always aware of, an incandescence in the trousers.

Whether Mr. Wise Guy can be imagined to say "perpetually effective" later in this stanza, or "forgotten all nomenclature" at the end of the stanza that follows is another question; Zukofsky's mask stays in place no more firmly than a mask of Swift's. By stanza four either the speaker has mutated or he's talked himself clear up to the highfalutin:

> Scarcely sojournin' in one place tho ever
> You'll see that he was where worthy folk throve; the
> New love, the quality 't has, moves to such sighing
> So that descrying the thing's place man causes
> Such clamour to rise, fired his passion pauses. . .

It's a notable moment when this flight drops suddenly back to the demotic:

> It don't go flying off to beds ov roses
> Nor cerrtainly to pick large or small posies.

"Posies" seems to have been prompted by the sound of Guido's *pocho*, "small":

> En non si mova
> > perch' a llui sir tirj
> E non s'aggirj
> > per trovari giocho
> E certamente gran saver nè pocho.

"And [Love] does not move, but makes all move toward it; and it does not bestir itself to look for pleasure, nor, certainly, for great knowledge nor small." Here Pound had first written,

> Love doth not move, but draweth all to him;
> Nor doth he turn
> > for a whim
> > > to find delight
> Nor to seek out, surely,
> > great knowledge or slight.

By 1934 Pound had reconsidered "knowledge"; in Canto XXXVI he wanted to align Guido firmly on the side of "proof by experiment," against the scholastic "knowledge" of "Aquinas head down in a vacuum"; and besides, the full experience of love is, ah, *physical:*

> Nor yet to seek out proving
> Be it so great or small.

This is delicately learned: "proving" in the old sense of "testing." (And it means? That Love doesn't sleep around?) Zukofsky slips in "prove" a little earlier, right where Guido has "che nol prova," and lets his stanza end with a worldly-wise wink:

> No one can know its likeness who don't prove the
> Face, love won't move tho it draws t' himself, aye 'n'
> It don't go flying off to beds ov roses
> Nor cerrtainly to pick large or small posies.

(That grotesque "aye 'n' " rhymes with "flying," also with "sighing.")

In the "Foin lass" the splended audacities—"Provin its boith or the responsible party," with an overtone of paternity suits; "Sumthin' to be seen by any smarty"; "You can't stand making friends with everybody" (Pound: "To stand with other / hast thou no desire")—are what strike at first reading. For the rest, the version is so infolded its cheekiness emerges slowly, under prodding, aided by diligent comparison with what's to be found in two books by Ezra Pound, notably the Guido text, the homage in Canto XXXVI, and the other Ezratical version with its dedication to the ghosts of

Campion and Lawes. In this "Foin lass" resembles the normative Zukofsky poem, which contains so much more than it seems to have room for. By some miracle of fourth-dimensional topology, Zukofsky routinely folded universes into matchboxes. He was content to let the initial impression seem to fall far short of poetry's promise, the reader's disappointed eye discerning merely the cube at the core of the hypercube. Time and thought attend a slow unfolding, and we may find ourselves looking up words we thought we knew, even "a" and "the." This experience too fluoresces in the light of Guido's dismissal of all save "persone ch anno intendimento": "You can't stand making friends with everybody."

To Louis Zukofsky

Charles Tomlinson

The morning
spent in

copying
your poems

from *Anew*
because that

was more
than any

publisher would
do for one,

was a
delight: I

sat high
over Taos

on a
veranda

Lawrence had
made in

exile here
exile

from those
who knew

how to write
only the way they

had been
taught to:

I put aside
your book

not tired
from copying but

wishing for
the natural complement

to all the
air and openness

such art
implied:

I went
remembering that

solitude
in the world

of letters
which is yours

taking
a mountain trail

and thinking
is not

poetry
akin to walking

for one
may know

the way that
he is going

(though I did not)
without

his knowing
what he

will see there:
and who

following on
will find

what you
with more than

walker's care
have shown

was there
before his

unaccounting eyes?

ZUK & EZ AT ST. LIZ

David Gordon

Janequin's gleeful bird song rose from Paul's violin, stirring Pound to deepest reverie, and then he bowed the patterns of Bach's Partita #3, with Rode-precision; Paul's concert renewing old poetry between the two old friends. After the Zukofskys left Ezra went through *Anew*, underscoring some of his favorite passages, "This science is then like gathering flowers of the weed." "I am like another, and another, who has / finished learning / and has just begun to learn." "Patiently bothering." "In the granite columns / that derive unwieldy acanthus." "Or of snow melting from trees / If it falls with a sound of leaves." "Distrust is cast off, all / cowardice dies. Eyes, looking out, / without the good of intellect." "And in a world from which most / ideas have gone / To take the wreck of its idea." "There are almost no friends / But a few birds to tell what you have done." "Past slate rock / you will see what soft blue is / with the sea / such eyes as you have." "Who must be like myself and not pity me / (I am, after all, of the people whose wisdom / May die with them)." Pound's quiet homage (7-11-54) to LZ.

THE PERSON

J. LAUGHLIN

who writes my poems
lives in some other

sphere he sends them
to me through space

when he feels like it
they arrive complete

from beginning to end
and all I have to do

is type them out who
is that person what is

he to me I wonder about
him but will never know.

NOTES ON CONTRIBUTORS

WALTER ABISH is the author of a collection of poems, *Duel Site,* and three books of fiction published by New Directions. A segment of an on-going work of fiction, "The Idea of Switzerland," will appear in *Partisan Review,* and part of "Self-Portrait," appearing in these pages, will be brought out in *Sub Stance: A Review of Theory and Literary Criticism.*

Biographical information on CARLOS DRUMMOND DE ANDRADE is given in the introduction to "Song for That Man of the People, Charlie Chaplin." GIOVANNI PONTIERO teaches in the Department of Spanish and Portuguese Studies at the University of Manchester. He is the author of a critical study of the Brazilian writer Nélida Piñon, and his translation of her story "Natural Frontier" appeared in *ND37.*

GREGORY CORSO, who will observe his fiftieth birthday in 1980, first won national attention in the 1950s as a leading spokesman of the Beat Generation. He has since published several books of poetry under the New Directions and City Lights imprints. His novel, *The American Express,* was published by Olympia Press, Paris, and a short play, *In This Hung-up Age,* appeared in *ND18.*

A professor of English at the University of California at San Diego, BRAM DIJKSTRA is the author of *The Hieroglyphics of a New Speech: Cubism, Stieglitz and the Early Poetry of William Carlos Williams* (1969). More recently, he compiled, edited, and introduced *A Recognizable Image: William Carlos Williams on Art and Artists,* published by New Directions in 1978.

For biographical information on JAIME GIL DE BIEDMA, see the translator's note preceding his "Eight Poems." LOUIS BOURNE, whose latest book is *Medula de la Llama* (*"Marrow of the Flame"*) is an American poet and translator living in Madrid.

YVAN GOLL was born in 1891 of French parents and brought up in Metz, then under German rule. With the advent of World War I, he fled to Switzerland and later to Paris, where he worked with James Joyce on the German translation of *Ulysses*. When France fell in 1940, he moved to New York, where he founded the French-American magazine *Hémisphères*. His *Jean sans terre* (*"Landless Jim"*) was translated into English by William Carlos Williams in 1944. "The Chapliniad," appearing here for the first time in English, is translated by FRANK JONES, whose rendering of Goll's "Paris Georgics" appeared in *ND34*. Jones, who teaches English and Comparative Literature at the University of Washington, has translated Euripides, Gide, Horace, Lucian, and—in collaboration with Simon Mpondo—David Mandessi Diop. His translation of Bertolt Brecht's *Saint Joan of the Stockyards* (Indiana University Press, 1970) won a National Book Award in 1971.

Educated in Egypt, Massachusetts, and California, CHRISTINE L. HEWITT has published two stories in *The North American Review*, and one ("Snow and Ice") in *ND37*. She is now working on a novel.

DAWSON JACKSON is English and lives in London. He has published two books of prose, but his life's work is writing verse, which he circulates chiefly among his friends. A collection, *Ice and the Orchard*, was published by Carcanet Press. He earns his living, he says, in as little of the year as need be, as a free-lance translator in Geneva and various other parts of the world.

J. LAUGHLIN's most recent book of poems is *In Another Country*, a selection made by Robert Fitzgerald and published by City Lights Books (1978).

New Directions published JOE ASHBY PORTER's novel *Eelgrass* in 1977. His most recent book, published by the University of California Press, is *The Drama of Speech Acts*. "In the Mind's Eye" is one of a group of stories set in his home state of Kentucky.

HOWARD STERN, born in 1947, is a writer and collagist who teaches German at Columbia University.

Much of the original material in "Tributes to Louis Zukovsky" originally appeared in *Paideuma* (Winter 1978). LOUIS ZUKOVSKY (1904–1978) was born in New York City. He received an M.A. from Columbia University in 1925 and taught at various universities and, until his retirement in 1966, at the Polytechnic Institute of Brooklyn. An editor, critic, and, in collaboration with his wife CELIA ZUKOVSKY, translator of Catullus, his major poetic work is the largely autobiographical sequence "A," begun in 1928 and completed in 1974, and published for the first time in its entirety last year by the University of California Press. BASIL BUNTING and GEORGE OPPEN were "co-students" with Zukovsky at Ezra Pound's "Ezuversity" in Rapallo. Oxford University Press brought out Bunting's *Collected Poems* in 1978. Oppen's *On Being Numerous,* published by New Directions, won the Pulitzer Prize for Poetry in 1969, and is included in his *Collected Poems.* The poet RONALD JOHNSON has written a book entitled *RADI OS,* published by the Sand Dollar Press at Berkeley. ROBERT CREELEY's *Later,* his newest book of poems, is being published by New Directions this fall. Scholar and critic HUGH KENNER teaches at Johns Hopkins University. His most recent book is *Joyce's Voices,* published by the University of California Press. HAYDEN CARRUTH is a prolific editor, critic, and poet; he is the author of the introduction to Jean-Paul Sartre's *Nausea,* and included among his many books of poetry are *For You* and *From Snow and Rock, From Chaos.* GUY DAVENPORT, the well-known critic, has long condemned the unwarranted reputation for obscurity of Zukovsky's work. The English poet and critic CHARLES TOMLINSON was born in 1927. His most recent book of poems is *The Shaft.* DAVID GORDON is a translator of Chinese poetry whose latest book is *Equinox: A Gathering of Tang Poets,* published by the Ohio University Press in 1975.

NEW BOOKS
BY RECENT CONTRIBUTORS

Spring 1979

THE WOMAN ON THE BRIDGE OVER THE CHICAGO RIVER / Allen Grossman. In his first collection with New Directions, Allen Grossman's often dissociated imagery borders on the surreal—yet one hears in his astonishingly contemporary voice classical and Biblical echoes and, on occasion, darker medieval undertones. The brilliance of his imagination works against a measured eloquence, setting up a fine-edged tension not unlike the prophetic verse of William Blake or the more controlled metrics of Catullus and Villon. Available clothbound and as New Directions Paperbook 473.

Fall 1979

LANDSCAPES OF LIVING & DYING / Lawrence Ferlinghetti. Because of his commitment to speak out on the condition of the contemporary "landscape," Ferlinghetti's work has, in the poet's words, a significant "public surface" while retaining its "subjective and/or subversive depth"—certainly a combination unique in poetry today. Many of these poems first appeared in the Op/Ed pages of metropolitan dailies across the nation. When the *San Francisco Examiner* published "An Elegy to Dispel Gloom," it justifiably named Ferlinghetti the "poet laureate of San Francisco." Available clothbound and as NDP491, as well as in a signed, limited edition.

A DRAFT OF SHADOWS AND OTHER POEMS / Octavio Paz. In a recent interview Paz stated: "When I am writing a poem, it is to make something, an object or organism that will be whole and living, something that will have a life independent of me." For Mexico's leading poet and essayist, poetry is a way of reinventing the self, and appropriately, the reflective title poem "A Draft of Shadows" concludes: "I am the shadow my words cast." This bilingual selection was edited by Eliot Weinberger, who worked closely with Paz on many of the selections. Elizabeth Bishop and Mark Strand supplied additional translations. Available clothbound and as NDP498.